I0731088

Love Me Please

Chris Bedell

This book is a work of fiction. Names, characters, places, and incidents are the product of the author's imagination or are used fictitiously. Any resemblance to actual events, locales, or persons, living or dead, is coincidental.

Copyright © 2021 Chris Bedell

Cover Design by Suzanne Johnson

Between the Lines Publishing and its imprints supports the right to free expression and the value of copyright. The scanning, uploading, and distribution of this book without permission is a theft of the author's intellectual property. If you would like permission to use material from the book (other than for review purposes), please contact info@btwnthelines.com.

Between the Lines Publishing
9 North River Road #248
Auburn, ME 04210
btwnthelines.com

First Published: February 2022

Willow River Press is an imprint of Between the Lines Publishing. The Liminal Books name and logo are trademarks of Between the Lines Publishing.

ISBN: 978-1-950502-65-3 (paperback)
ISBN: 978-1-950502-66-0 (eBook)

The publisher is not responsible for websites (or their content) that are not owned by the publisher.

Love Me
Please

CHAPTER 1

Everyone loved Declan Price.

Including his fellow players on the football team. And the cheerleaders. And the nerds. And even the students in the chess club.

I couldn't help doubting my friendship with Declan, though. I stood in his empty guest bedroom, sipping a cocktail from my Solo cup. Music pulsed through the air from an adjacent room while I glanced at the encyclopedia set in the bookcase.

Declan convinced me to attend his party tonight, but I couldn't find him anywhere in the mansion. I even texted him a few times. But he didn't return any of my messages.

Whatever. At least I left the house for once. Better than being stuck in my bedroom watching Netflix on a Friday night.

Something in my pocket vibrated, then I put my drink on the table by the bookshelf. I took my iPhone from my pocket. My throat burned after I checked the Caller ID. Mom was calling.

I exhaled a long breath. Answering Mom's call was better than avoiding her. It was simpler this way.

"Hello," I said.

"Where the fuck are you, Colton?" Mom asked, slurring her words.

"I went for a drive."

"Don't lie to me, you ungrateful little shit. I can see your car in the driveway."

"How much have you had to drink?"

"Only a couple glasses of gin."

I scratched the back of my neck with my free hand. "Go to bed and sleep it off. You'll feel better in the morning."

"Don't tell me what to do!" Mom exclaimed, causing brief static on her end of the line.

Mom shouldn't have played the adult card. It wasn't like she ever did anything worth respecting. She never would. If she couldn't be kind to her son, then there wasn't much hope for her being decent.

I rolled my eyes. "Tell me what you want."

"I know you went to Declan Price's party."

"Excuse me?"

"Don't lie. I saw the Facebook page he created for the event," Mom said.

I bit my lip. Fear filled my insides while I considered what to say next. So much for lying my way out of this situation.

"Why'd you ask me a question you already know the answer to?" I asked.

"I was testing you."

"I don't have to justify my life to you."

"I hope attending the party is worth it." Mom paused for a beat. "Because I'm gonna beat the fucking shit out of you when you get home."

Shock should've trickled through my body. But it didn't. This conversation wasn't the first time she threatened to beat me. It wasn't even the worst thing she'd ever said to me.

I snorted. "You won't even remember this conversation."

"Don't be an asshole."

"Go to bed."

"You've got a lot of nerve attending the party," Mom said. "I told you to avoid him. He's a bad influence. You didn't start acting weird until you met Declan. It's his fault you're a faggot."

I fought back the tears despite being alone in the room. Some truths couldn't be processed no matter how simple they were. Like how Mom was ashamed of me even though it should've been the other way around. Having a drunk for a mother wasn't exactly fun.

"I've gotta go," I said.

She hissed. "Don't you dare! We're done when I say we are."

"I'm not afraid of you."

"You used to be a much better liar."

"Bye, Mom. And please don't drive anywhere tonight."

"If you come home right now, then I'll only burn you with a cigarette for fifteen seconds instead of thirty."

"Bye." I pressed END, then tucked my iPhone into my pocket.

Hanging up on Mom was the least she deserved. I needed to do something for myself. Something that showed I wasn't submissive to her. Something that might not make me cry myself to sleep. Something that'd make me forget about the last seventeen years of my life.

I sobbed. No harm in letting myself feel my current sadness. Not lying to myself was important even if I wasn't capable of being honest with anyone else. If I bottled my emotions for too long, then I might explode.

The door creaked. A guy with spiked hair stood by the bedroom's entrance.

"Sorry. Thought this was the bathroom." Tripp tugged at the sides of his varsity jacket.

"No worries," I mumbled.

Tripp furrowed an eyebrow. "Everything okay?"

"I'm fine." I grabbed my Margarita, then chugged the rest of it. The tequila's distinct taste burned my throat while I licked my lips, savoring the sweet and lime flavors. I squashed my cup, letting it fall onto the ground.

Tripp's jaw twitched. "You don't seem fine."

"The bathroom is down the hall." I shuffled towards the bed before sitting on it.

The door clinked after Tripp locked it. He joined me on the bed.

Tripp chuckled. "Something happen?"

I looked away. "It's a long story."

"I'm a good listener."

"Thanks."

Tripp placed his hands on his lap. "We lost the football game, and I'm still in a good mood. So, I'm sure your problem can't be that bad."

Most people might have been pissed at Tripp for making an assumption if they were me. But I wasn't. Tripp was taking an interest in my life, and that was more than could be said for most people.

Tripp met my gaze. "I promise I won't judge."

"I believe you."

"This is the most we've ever talked."

"So?"

"I just meant you never speak up in class."

"I don't have anything important to say," I said.

He winked. "You're wrong."

"Huh?"

"The quiet ones are the most insightful people." He patted my shoulder.

I didn't push his hand away, though. Something comforting existed from him touching me. Maybe, just maybe, this is what being human entailed. Experiencing a little kindness. Something to show I wasn't alone.

I sucked on my teeth. "You don't have to stay. I'm sure you'd rather be flirting with some cheerleader."

"I'm gay, Colt."

I almost gave Tripp a dirty look. I wasn't sure how I was supposed to feel about someone giving me a nickname—nobody ever called me, "Colt" before. Tripp could've been trying to connect with me. Or he could've been too forward. Not everyone liked nicknames, after all.

Tripp wiggled his eyebrows. "Did you hear me? I'm gay."

"Cool," I said.

Tripp laughed louder this time. "Maybe you missed my big coming out during sophomore year."

"Yeah."

Tripp's smile widened. "Great shirt by the way. The blue brings out your eyes."

How kind of Tripp. It wasn't like Mom ever said anything nice to me. In fact, silence was a gift with Mom. At least then we wouldn't argue. Only so many bruises could be blamed on clumsiness. I would've been lying to myself if I didn't acknowledge how several of my teachers had gotten suspicious of my injuries over the years.

"Thanks," I said.

"What? Aren't you gonna give me a compliment?" he asked.

I almost choked. I didn't realize I was expected to say something nice back. It wasn't like I bullied him into praising me.

"I'm kidding," Tripp said.

My mouth gaped. "Oh."

"Don't socialize much, do you?"

"You can leave. I promise I'm okay."

"Trying to get rid of me?" Tripp asked.

My stomach lurched. As much as I wanted to be a jerk; I couldn't. I wanted this moment with Tripp.

I glanced at Tripp. "I mean, you can stay if you want. Doesn't matter—nothing does."

Tripp's face lit up. "I know something that'll make you feel better."

"I'll try anything."

"But you've gotta close your eyes."

"Come again?" I asked.

"Do you trust me?"

I nodded.

"Then close your eyes," Tripp said.

Deep breaths. It wasn't like Tripp could be worse than Mom. Nothing could. She took the prize for cruelest human alive.

So, I closed my eyes.

Something brushed up against my lips. Judging by the smooth, cotton-like texture, Tripp must've kissed me. He started giving tongue, so I did the only thing I could. I opened my mouth more, letting Tripp stick his tongue further inside my mouth. I pushed my tongue against his. Tripp placed his hands on my cheeks, and the sweet and earthly scent of whatever cologne Tripp used wafted through the air, tickling my nostrils.

My pulse should've hammered in my ears, yet it didn't. For once, I was where I belonged. I deserved to do more things for myself. Nobody else would fight for my happiness like I would. Even if Mom disapproved of me making out with a boy.

Tripp pulled away, then I opened my eyes.

"Well?" he demanded.

"Interesting," I said.

"Fantastic. Exactly the reaction I wanted."

I remained silent.

He nudged me. "Feel better?"

"Yeah."

Tripp continued staring at me. My stomach twisted in ten different directions. I didn't know it was possible to have such intense eye contact with someone. That kind of thing was something that only seemed possible in movies and television shows.

"Gotta be back home by a certain time?" Tripp asked.

"Nope."

Mom would be passed out beyond drunk on the couch within an hour or two. So, no point in returning home this evening. It wasn't like Mom could do anything terrible to me tonight.

"Good," Tripp said. "Because I've got an idea about what we could do next."

"Cool."

Tripp inhaled a breath. "If you're interested, that is."

"Absolutely."

CHAPTER 2

I opened the front door the following afternoon, then entered my house. Mom was sitting on the living room couch, and a bottle of gin and empty glass were in front of her on the wooden, coffee table.

My heart almost leapt out of my chest while I walked over to her. Best to get her anger over with. Nothing she did changed what happened to me last night, because that was one thing she couldn't steal from me.

"Little early in the day to be drinking," I said.

She looked up at me. "If I wanted your opinion, then I'd ask for it."

"Your car was in a different spot then when I left last night. Please tell me you didn't drive drunk?"

"None of your fucking business." Mom ran her fingers through her brown hair before pouring herself another glass of gin. She chugged her drink in a matter of seconds, then belched. "You didn't sleep in your bed last night."

I folded my arms. "I don't answer to you."

Her lips curled. "I'd watch yourself if I were you. You're lucky I'm not beating you for your disobedience."

"Okay."

"I'm actually drinking to celebrate."

I sneered. "What's the occasion? Going an hour without a drink?"

"I'll let that go."

"You aren't gonna bitch about last night?" I asked.

"Nope."

I didn't respond. Instead, my jaw twitched. Disbelief flooded my body. Mom couldn't have granted me a reprieve. That was like saying the solar system revolved around Mars.

"Declan Price is dead," Mom blurted.

"Come again?"

"I'm serious. Check your phone if you don't believe me."

I pulled my phone from my pocket. Then, I went on Safari before going to *The Lakewood Press's* website. Someone must've ripped out my intestines and wrapped them around my throat. Mom wasn't lying. The first story at the top of the page was about Declan's death. He was discovered shot in the head in the woods behind his house. No official cause of death, but the police suspect he was drunk and accidentally shot himself while playing with one of his father's guns.

Guilt crept through my body. Here I was, pissed at Declan for not keeping me company at his party last night. And now he was dead. Tears welled in my eyes while I clenched my fist.

I clicked my phone off before shoving it inside my pocket. I couldn't believe it. My only friend at Lakewood High School was dead.

Mom smirked. "Something wrong?"

"I'm fine."

Showing weakness in front of Mom was the last thing I could do. That'd be worse than having an emotional breakdown at school. I couldn't let Mom know she succeeded with breaking me. I deserved some dignity, at least.

"You can cry if you want," Mom said.

"I'm good."

Mom rose, then wrapped her arms around me. The acrid stench of the gin on her breath prickled my skin while goosebumps formed on my arms, back, and legs. Nothing comforting existed from Mom touching me. It was the exact opposite of Tripp clapping my shoulder last night.

"I'm sorry if I'm tough on you, but it's for your own good," Mom said. "You deserve the best, and we can't have people thinking certain things about you."

"Whatever you say."

She adjusted my collar. "You'll thank me someday."

"Okay."

Mom released me. "I'm not a monster. I have sympathy for Declan's parents. No parent deserves to bury their child. I wouldn't wanna return from a weekend getaway to discover my child died."

"How kind of you."

"I don't want you going to his funeral." Mom took out a pack of cigarettes and lighter from her pocket. She yanked a cigarette from the pack and lit it. After that, she took a drag and exhaled a thick cloud of smoke.

"I wish you wouldn't smoke inside," I said.

"Not like I'm gonna start a fire."

"Not intentionally, at least."

"What's that supposed to mean?" Mom exhaled a bigger drag this time, blowing the smoke in my face.

I coughed. What a fucking bitch. She could've shown more consideration. "Are we good?" I asked.

"Yeah." She gripped her cigarette tighter. "But I'm not clueless."

"The fuck is that supposed to mean?"

"I can smell the cologne on you."

"So?" I asked.

Maintaining my composure was essential. Mom could never know what happened last night. Nobody could. It was for the best. If there was one thing I learned in life, it was that what teachers and adults told kids in elementary school about anything being possible was a big fucking lie. I couldn't be whatever I wanted to be. Not when I had a mother who judged me before I even got up in the morning.

"You don't wear cologne," Mom said.

"And your point is?"

"You were obviously with someone."

"You've got no proof."

"And that's why I'm not gonna put this cigarette out on you." Mom took one final drag, then stubbed her cigarette on the ashtray next to her glass and gin bottle. "Not this time, at least."

"If you've got something to say, then say it," I said.

"I didn't see anything, so I'm good."

I narrowed my gaze. "You never told me where you went last night."

"None of your fucking business. For once, everything is right with the universe."

"Whatever."

Mom placed her hands on her hips. "Shouldn't you be at school?"

It was official. Mom was a bigger fucking idiot than a repeat senior. Knowing the day of the week shouldn't have been so easy to fuck up. It wasn't like she had dementia.

"It's Saturday."

She gasped. "Oh…"

"Cutting back on the booze might help your memory."

Mom made a pig-like snort. "Please."

"I'm serious."

"It might not be a school day, but I assume you've got homework."

"I did it yesterday during my free periods," I spat.

It was a minor victory, but I earned it. Here Mom was, expecting the worst from me. But no. She was wrong. And I'd hold onto said fact. Being petty and internally gloating was pretty much the only fulfillment I got out of life.

"I still want you out of my sight," Mom said.

"Fine by me."

"If you behave yourself, then we can order a pizza for dinner."

"Great." I walked away from her without another word before ascending the staircase to my bedroom.

Minor gloating wasn't the only thing I had. I could also be thankful for my own room. Something, anything to give me a minor reprieve from Mom's belligerence.

I grabbed my textbooks and notebooks from my locker Monday morning before first period when someone tapped my shoulder.

I spun around. Tripp stood in front of me.

Tripp gave me a small smile. "I assume you heard about Declan? I'm so sorry. I know he was kind of your only friend here."

I closed my locker, then zipped my backpack.

Tripped sighed. "I don't mean to bother you, but I was wondering if you'd like to hang. Maybe go on a date."

I dug my fingernails into my backpack straps, yanking them up more. I didn't speak. I just continued holding eye contact with Tripp.

"I had a lot of fun the other night, and it'd be cool to get to know you," Tripp said.

My chest expanded and contracted while my pulse increased. Tripp couldn't be doing this. Not here. Not at school. Nobody could uncover my secret about how I was bisexual.

He pressed his hands together. "Did I say something wrong?"

"Get the fuck away from me, you fucking loser faggot."

Tripp's Adam's apple throbbed. "I didn't mean to offend you."

Sweat clung to my brow, and I grabbed Tripp by his varsity jacket's collar before punching him. Not having anyone know I liked guys was the only thing that mattered in this moment. Even if I wished the exact opposite was true. Like with how I would've loved to date Tripp.

"What the hell is going on?" called out a voice.

Tripp bopped me with his head, then shoved me off him. Mr. Hopper, the man who just yelled at us and happened to be our math teacher, scurried towards us.

Mr. Hopper crossed his arms, wrinkling his gray blazer. "Now isn't the time to be fighting. Especially after what happened to Declan."

"This was my fault," Tripp said. "The only reason Colton attacked me was because I provoked him."

I must've had earwax stuck in my ears. Tripp couldn't be lying for me. Not after I attacked him. I didn't deserve kindness from Tripp. I wouldn't have been generous if I was in his position. No reason to help someone who revealed their psycho side.

"Go on," Mr. Hopper said.

"I told him that Declan was never his friend, and was using him because he was bored," Tripp said.

Mr. Hopper rubbed his mustache. "Why'd you say that?"

"I grew distant from Declan," Tripp said.

Mr. Hopper glared at Tripp. "But you're both on the football team."

"Sports doesn't solve everything," Tripp said. "People drift apart."

Mr. Hopper coughed into his right arm. "I'll let it slide because of Declan dying, but if anything like this happens again, I'm giving you detention."

Phew. I didn't know what I would've done if Mr. Hopper gave us detention. I couldn't put a positive spin on that for Mom. She'd probably burn me with a cigarette and spew some shit about how that would inspire me to do better and never get detention again.

"Understood," Tripp said.

Mr. Hopper shifted his attention towards me.

"Whatever," I murmured.

Mr. Hopper darted away from us, then Tripp shuffled down the hallway in the opposite direction, leaving me alone.

I kicked my feet against the ground while students and teachers flocked through the hallway when the warning bell rang a moment later. I couldn't believe it. Declan dying and having a physically abusive drunk for a mother wasn't bad enough. I ruined my connection with the one person who showed me kindness, and regret washed over me. So now, I'd just have to live with the consequences of my actions.

CHAPTER 3

I sat at a table in the back of VERONICA'S late Wednesday afternoon.

Grabbing coffee with an old friend shouldn't have been a big deal, yet I couldn't stop the nervous tapping of my feet against the tile floor.

The placard on the door jingled, then high heels scraped the ground. A girl with auburn hair strutted into the coffee shop and approached my table.

Gina clapped her hands. "Great to see you, Colton."

"You too."

"Sorry about the delay. Traffic was a bitch."

I feigned a smile. "No worries."

She giggled. "Don't just stand there. Aren't you gonna hug me?"

"Sure." I stood, then Gina hugged me before I could blink. If I didn't know better, I would've thought an elephant wanted to crush my windpipe. But no. Gina was just showing her love. Apparently, some people believed hugs were as important as oxygen.

"I'm so glad we're doing this." Gina ruffled my hair.

I glared at her. "What did I tell you about messing up my hair?"

She raised her palms at me. "Sorry."

"Don't worry about it."

"That's more like it." Gina surveyed our table, then resumed eye contact.

"Wanna place our orders?"

Gina removed her jacket, then put it on the back of the chair. "Sure."

I took my wallet out.

"What are you doing?" she asked.

"I was gonna treat."

"You wish."

"Excuse me?" I asked.

"I was the one who asked you to coffee, so my treat."

"You don't have to. I can pay for myself."

She exhaled a breath. "It's the least I can do after what happened to Declan. Can't imagine what you must be going through."

It felt nice for Gina to do something for me. I couldn't remember the last time Mom bought something for me that wasn't groceries. And Mom's coldness irritated me big time. It wasn't like I asked to be born — she was the one who brought me into the world. So, it would've been nice if she pretended to care a little. It wasn't like I wanted diamonds and a Mercedes.

"Thanks," I said.

"Besides, we haven't hung out since Memorial Day sophomore year."

"And now it's October of senior year."

Gina tucked a lock of hair behind her ear. "I didn't anticipate how private school would mean less time for my childhood bestie."

"Don't worry about it."

"I really am sorry if it seems like I've been blowing you off," Gina said.

"No worries. Not your fault your parents wanted you to go to a private school, so you'd have a better chance of getting into an elite college."

Gina picked her nail. "Still like your caramel latte?"

I nodded.

"And with whipped cream and caramel drizzle?" Gina asked.

"You better believe it."

"I'll be right back," Gina said.

"Sounds good."

Gina returned to our table several minutes later and handed me my mug before sitting in her chair.

"You can vent if you want. I'd love the distraction," Gina said.

I scoffed. "Seriously?"

"Yeah, absolutely."

"Good to know." I placed my lips and devoured the whipped cream and caramel drizzle.

Gina squeezed my hand. "It's okay to be sad. Nobody would blame you for that."

"Life is just so fleeting." I curled my fingers into a brief fist, fighting back tears. In theory I knew there was nothing wrong with crying, yet I was still in public. "One minute Declan was alive, and the next he was dead. And he was basically just a kid."

"Shit. Maybe we need to hang more. You're too young to be cynical."

The placard clinked against the door, and I cocked my head. A group of guys in varsity jackets just entered VERONICA'S. I was more concerned with the guy I locked eyes with, though. More specifically, Tripp. He and his friends just walked by my table.

My throat tightened. Mom's words and actions weren't the only thing that would remain burned in my mind for the foreseeable future. I couldn't forget about punching Tripp and how I wanted nothing more than to apologize for our altercation on Monday.

Gina leaned closer. "What the hell was that about?"

I sipped my caramel latte. "Nothing."

"I'm not that gullible. I saw the look you guys exchanged."

"Leave it alone!" I exclaimed.

"Do you like him?" she whispered.

"Gina, please!"

"I'm not judging. I have a gay uncle."

"Cool."

Gina squealed at me. "I'm serious. That glance isn't the way you'd look at a friend."

I resisted making a fist or screaming; it would've been a shame to throw over ten years of friendship away just because discussing my sexuality made me uncomfortable.

"If there's something you wanna tell me, then don't hold back," Gina continued.

"I'm bisexual," I blurted, making sure not to speak too loudly.

Relief trickled through my body. For one moment, my life wasn't a warzone. I told Gina my truth and said fact fucking mattered. I couldn't help feeling great. I let someone in, and my life hadn't imploded. So, maybe there was hope for me yet.

She took a larger sip of her mocha latte. "Makes no difference to me what you are. Just want you to be happy."

"Thanks."

"I'm serious, Colton."

My heart thumped louder and louder. I still couldn't deny how telling Gina my secret felt great. Yet the feeling of being on edge wasn't something that would go away as long as I had my mother to contend with.

Gina picked her nail. "I haven't been honest with you. Declan's death wasn't the only reason I wanted to catch up."

"Come again?"

"I heard about your fight with Tripp."

"How?" I demanded.

"A lot of kids from Lakewood High are friends with students at Fulton Prep."

"Oh."

Her eyebrows knitted together. "How could you punch someone? What if you got suspended? Expelled? Or even arrested?"

Gina was always this dramatic. Violence was generally a bad thing, but nothing bad happened to me from my fight with Tripp.

"I didn't," I said.

"Because you got lucky," Gina interrupted.

"It's not like Tripp needed medical attention."

"Are you kidding?" she asked.

"I wasn't trying to kill him."

"You've got to be careful," Gina said. "If you leave your temper unchecked, then you might hurt someone."

"Thanks, Mom."

"This isn't a game, Colton."

"Okay."

Gina's eyes bulged. "Perhaps your mother is the reason for your stress? I know you two never got along. Is she the reason you don't wanna come out?"

Creepy. It was as if Gina saw through me.

That was the nature of a best friend, though. The amount of time between interactions didn't matter. A real friend could always detect bullshit. So, there was a good chance Gina was gonna make me deal with my feelings whether I wanted to or not.

"You're making a lot of assumptions," I said.

"They were just questions."

"Let's change the subject."

Gina rolled her sleeves up. "What the hell happened between you and Tripp?"

"It's complicated."

"Good thing I've got plenty of time because I'm not leaving until you tell me what happened."

The laughter from Tripp's table at the opposite end of the coffee shop grew louder. And I couldn't help thinking back to Declan's party right after Tripp and I kissed.

Tripp and I remained seated on the bed.

I just told him I was interested in whatever he wanted to do next. And for once in my life, I wasn't lying. Perhaps Tripp could take away my pain for a moment or two. Tripp also seemed like a genuinely nice guy. Most people wouldn't give one shit to let someone vent at a party.

"Why don't we lay down on the bed?" Tripp asked.

"Sure."

We got down on the bed, then scooted upward. Tripp's eyes remained glued on me, and my stomach was tighter than any rope knot. I just wasn't used to getting so much attention before.

"I know something else that'll feel even better than kissing," Tripp said.

"Cool."

"Still trust me?"

I didn't know whether to grunt or smile at Tripp's formalness. I wasn't some delicate virgin from the eighteenth century. Yet something comforting existed from Tripp constantly checking to making sure I was still interested. It was the only time anyone ever cared about what I wanted. I couldn't deny that having my needs matter was nice.

"Well?" Tripp continued.

"I trust you."

"Good." Tripp placed his hands on my waist, then yanked my basketball shorts and plaid boxers to my ankles. He surveyed my waist then returned eye contact.

I nodded.

Tripp moved his attention back to my waist, and his head started bobbing forward and backward. I moaned while digging my fingers into Tripp's hair. Damn. I didn't realize it was possible to feel this good.

Tripp pulled his head away from my body then smirked at me. "Well?"

"Holy shit!" I exclaimed, clouded by a euphoric feeling. I just never once realized how giving into a basic pleasure—like sex—could feel so good. I'd never felt this good before.

Tripp smirked. "I do aim to please."

"Don't get cocky."

"Wanna come back to my house?" Tripp asked. "My parents are away for the weekend."

I chuckled, then he fretted.

"I'm not making fun of you," I said. "Just kind of weird how both yours and Declan's parents are away for the weekend."

Tripp chuckled. "That's rich people for you."

Jealousy shot through my body for a split second despite how Tripp hadn't said anything damning. I wanted nothing more than to have a carefree life. More specifically, a parent that loved and supported me.

But no. I was Colton Foster. The kid who was barely surviving. The kid who wondered if he had a future. The kid who wondered what terrible thing he did to deserve an abusive mother. Because to say that I was overwhelmed would've been an underestimate.   .

Tripp cupped my chin. "What are you thinking about?"

Ranting to Tripp about my insecurities wouldn't happen no matter how sympathetic he was. Nothing like ranting to ruin the mood. Besides, maybe I could will myself to be happy. At least while I was

Tripp, that was. If I thought I was enjoying myself, then I might actually have fun.

"I'd love to go to your house," I said.

"Great. Did you drive here?"

"I took an UBER. Why?"

"Looks like I'll be driving you then." He paused for a second. "If that's okay with you."

"What do you mean?" I asked.

"Nothing. Forget it," Tripp said. "Do you wanna leave this room together or would you rather me go first and you meet me at my car in ten minutes?"

"The former."

The adrenaline rush from giving myself permission to be myself intoxicated me. My happiness was the only thing that mattered tonight, and I wouldn't have it any other way. My encounter with Tripp would be over before I knew it, so I'd have to enjoy every minute while I could.

Tripp and I stood in his bedroom sometime later.

"I hope you like my bedroom," Tripp said.

"It's nice."

"Thanks."

The papers were stacked neatly on his desk, there wasn't so much as one clump of dust on his bookcase, and all his dirty clothes were in his hamper. And that was more than could be said for most teens, including myself. My clothes were lucky if they made it into my drawers, because I had better things to do than fold my clothing. Like wondering if I'd ever escape Mom. I wanted nothing more than to cut her out of my life once and for all.

"So," I stammered.

Tripp rocked his hands back and forth. "We can just make out some more and watch a movie. It's okay if you've changed your mind."

"I'm a big boy, and can look after myself."

His face drooped.

"But thank you," I continued. "The kindness is refreshing."

"No problem." Tripp kissed me, yet I didn't close my eyes this time.

I wanted to experience every second of making out with him. Like inhaling the pleasant smell of whatever cologne he used. Or his tongue massaging my mouth. Or his smooth hands brushing up against my cheeks.

Tripp pulled back a moment later.

"Now what?" I asked.

"I haven't done this in a long time."

"It's okay for you to change your mind too," I said.

"It's not that."

"Then what?" I asked.

"Don't laugh."

I shook my head. "I won't."

"Escaping the loneliness is nice."

"But you're on the football team, and are one of the most popular guys at Lakewood High," I said.

He rubbed his forehead. "That isn't everything."

"I know something that'll make you feel better," I said.

Tripp winked. "Yeah?"

I kissed Tripp without giving the matter a second thought. It was my turn to massage his mouth with my tongue and grip his cheeks while we kissed even though the height difference might've been slightly awkward since he was several inches taller than me. Taking the initiative was important, though. I wanted this as much as he did.

We detached from the kiss a moment, grinning at each other. Wow. I never knew the feeling of having nothing else matter was possible.

"There are logistics to discuss," Tripp said.

I wrinkled my nose. "I'm not an idiot."

"Not to sound presumptuous, but it's probably safe to say I'm the dominant one in this situation. That okay with you?"

"Yup."

Tripp and I just kept staring at each other. I couldn't believe this. I was about to lose my virginity—finally have a more typical teen experience.

"Do you have everything we need?" I asked.

"In my top desk drawer."

"Nice."

"This is it, I guess?" Tripp asked.

"Yeah. We're really doing this."

Tripp's smirk expanded. "Awesome."

I kissed him without another word, and his hands traveled to my waist before lifting my tee-shirt off my body. Tripp tossed it on the floor, then I removed his shirt. We ditched our remaining clothes, and we were soon on his bed.

I tilted my head while Tripp's hands remained wrapped around mine. A scorching sensation jabbed my stomach, but not because I was angry. I just had never trusted myself to be vulnerable with someone before.

"Ready?" Tripp asked.

"Yes," I mumbled.

Tripp and I rolled onto our backs sometime later, then he scooted closer towards me, free hand resting under the left side of his head.

"So?" Tripp asked.

"It was nice."

"Good. I'm glad."

I opened my mouth, yet words escaped me. I didn't know what else to say.

Tripp beamed his eyes. "You're welcome to stay the night."

I nibbled on the inside of my lip. I just didn't know if Tripp only suggested I stay the night to be polite or if he actually enjoyed my company.

"That desperate for round two?" I asked.

"No."

"I was teasing."

Tripp let out a faint laugh. "I know."

"I'd love to stay the night. Not like I have anywhere else to be," I said.

Tripp caressed my head, messing up my hair.

"Watch the hair!" I exclaimed.

"If you're lucky, I'll even make you breakfast in bed tomorrow morning."

I couldn't swallow the lump in my throat. I was impressed with how Tripp seemed like a good person. Mom never made me breakfast before. Throwing a loaf of bread at me and telling me which setting to use on the toaster was the most maternal she ever was.

Another thought popped into my head. I just couldn't shake Tripp's behavior. While his kindness was refreshing, I wondered if he was slowly getting attached to me. Like maybe this wasn't only sex for him, and he wanted a real connection.

"I can't believe you lost your virginity before I did," Gina said, snapping me out of my tale.

"No big deal," I said.

Gina finished her mocha latte. "Don't be silly. Everyone remembers their first time."

"Could you sound more cliché?"

Gina whipped her head back and forth.

"It was a rhetorical question," I said.

"I know." Gina slid her elbows onto the table, then leaned closer. "Is it possible you wanted it to be more than a hookup?"

"Doesn't matter."

She grabbed my hands. "If you have regret, then you should apologize to Tripp."

I averted my focus to my chipped mug—I couldn't believe I still had half of my latte left. Usually, I would've finished my drink before Gina. "Not like he'll forgive me," I said.

"You'll never know unless you try."

"Nah. He probably hates me, and I don't blame him."

"I'm sure that's not true."

"You're the one who lectured me about punching him." I chugged the rest of my latte, not bothering to savor the mixture of the sweet caramel and bitter espresso.

"You didn't murder someone, you just punched someone. So, it's not like your life is over. If you want a second chance, then pursue it." Gina grunted. "If you don't give things with Tripp another shot, then I can't live vicariously through you."

The chattering of numerous voices filled the coffee shop. But I wouldn't worry about getting a headache from the loudness. Instead, I contemplated what Gina said about second chances. It was interesting, really. Debating who was and wasn't worthy of a do-over.

The only question that remained was if I was gonna be a coward or not. I already knew which option was easier.

CHAPTER 4

I approached Tripp the following morning in the school hallway.

"Do you have a sec?" I asked.

He raised his eyebrows. "Why would I ever talk to you?"

I pressed my hands together. "Please. It's important."

"You have five minutes."

I sighed in relief.

Sure. No guarantee Tripp would forgive me, but agreeing to talk was the first step. And that was enough for me. If he hated me, then he would've cussed me out and told me he never wanted to see me again.

I led Tripp into an empty adjacent hallway.

Tripp pulled his backpack straps up his shoulders. "What?"

"I wanna apologize. I'm sorry about punching you the other day. That was wrong, and you didn't deserve it, because you've been so nice to me."

Tripp didn't speak.

"I shouldn't have taken my anger out on you," I continued. "I don't expect you to forgive me. Just wanted to let you know I'm sorry."

"Stop," Tripp bellowed.

"Huh?"

"I forgive you."

I swallowed the lump in my throat. Perhaps life wasn't completely terrible—I hadn't expected Tripp's forgiveness. I still wasn't sure if I could be so generous if the situation was reversed. So, maybe, just maybe, there was hope for us.

"You do?" I asked.

He let out a breath. "You made a stupid mistake, and you don't deserve to be punished for the rest of your life."

"Can we start over?" I asked. "I'd love to go out on that date."

"No."

"You just said you forgive me."

"I meant what I said."

"Then what's the problem?" I asked.

"I can't be around you. It's obvious you have a lot of emotional baggage to deal with, and that's okay. Not everyone is ready to come out in high school. We had fun, and that's that."

Tears pricked my eyes. Disappointment filled my entire body. I expected Tripp to either forgive me or not, not forgive me but not wanna have anything to do with me.

Tripp bit his lip. "I'm not trying to hurt your feelings. I've just gotta look out for myself. It's senior year, and nothing can jeopardize my future."

"Sure," I forced out.

"Is that it?" he asked.

"You aren't being fair."

His eyes widened. "Come again?"

"I'm not a terrible person."

"Never said you were. But are you forgetting what happened the next morning?"

The faint shuffling of footsteps echoed from a nearby hallway, and I thought about the morning after Tripp, and I hooked up.

Sunlight poked through the bedroom curtains. I yawned, then opened my eyes. My heart even skipped several beats. Tripp wasn't in bed next to me.

Deep breaths. This was his house, so he'd have to return at some point. It wasn't like I'd never see him again.

The bedroom door burst open a moment later, and Tripp walked in with a tray, which consisted of two plates of pancakes, a bottle of maple syrup—the good kind, not the lite brand—and orange juice and silverware for the two of us.

Tripp put the tray down on the bed before joining me, careful not to knock over the tray. The way he moved was kind of cute. Making a mess in bed would've ruined the moment.

Tripp eyed me. "Morning."

"Morning."

Tripp gave me a quick peck on the lips.

I chuckled. "Thought you were joking about making me breakfast."

"I wouldn't kid about that."

"This was sweet of you."

"No big deal. Just pancakes."

I looked down at the bed comforter. "Nobody has ever made me breakfast before."

"I'm glad I could be your first in more than one way."

I took in several deep breaths. Smaller moments impacted my life just as much as big moments. I couldn't help getting choked up over something as little as having breakfast with the guy I hooked up with. Tripp was treating me like a human being, and that was worth everything in the world.

"Something wrong?" Tripp asked.

"Just allergies."

"It's October."

"So?" I demanded.

Tripp elbowed me. "Don't worry. Secret's safe with me. I won't tell anyone you have a soft side."

"Not sure what you're talking about."

"You should eat your food before it gets cold." Tripp cut a piece from my pancakes, dunked it in maple syrup, then fed it to me. "How is it?"

"Okay."

"That's it?" Tripp asked.

Tripp might've been more dramatic than I realized. This was breakfast, not brain surgery. Burning the pancakes would've been the only way to ruin them.

"What do you want me to say?" I asked.

"Only teasing." Tripp drank his orange juice. "Anyway, you should be flattered. I've never cooked for anyone before."

I wrinkled my nose. Tripp could've been trying to make a genuine effort, or this might've been a fuckboy move in hopes of me hooking up with him again.

"I'd sleep with you again even if you didn't make me breakfast," I said.

"Really?" he asked.

"Maybe."

Tripp wet his right index finger, then wiped my lower lip. His mouth was less than an inch from mine. And I wanted nothing more than to kiss him. But I wasn't sure if that would've ruined the moment.

"You had syrup on your lips," Tripp said.

"Thanks."

"Don't mention it." Tripp winked. "Go ahead. I know you wanna kiss me."

"Later. Let's finish breakfast first."

Tripp gave me a mock scowl. "Fine."

"Making breakfast isn't manual labor," I said.

Tripp locked his arms together. "It's not about the breakfast. It's about what the breakfast represents. I allowed myself to feel something, and you went ballistic."

"I said I was sorry. Maybe you're angrier than you realized."

"Not about being angry. I gotta look after myself, because we clearly aren't compatible."

The bell screeched.

"Goodbye, Colton." Tripp walked away from me.

Students flooded the hallway while I continued standing in my same spot. Whatever. I apologized, and there wasn't anything I could do about it.

Perhaps the universe did me a favor. Better for my dynamic with Tripp not to go any further. It wasn't like we could be real boyfriends. If we went on a date, then someone might spot us, and that someone might tattle to Mom.

I stood by the kitchen table afterschool, reading *The Lakewood Press*.

My chest tightened at the newspaper's headline. The police officially ruled Declan's death an accident, but I couldn't help my uneasy feeling. Declan wasn't clumsy enough to shoot himself. Even if he had a few drinks that night. He was the same person who never cheated on a test, never did steroids (even though half the students on the football team did), and waited till his parents were out of town to host a party.

Footsteps echoed, growing louder with each second. Mom entered the kitchen, smoking a cigarette.

She walked over to me, then glanced at the newspaper headline before blowing a cloud of smoke in my face. "Thought I told you to forget about Declan Price? He's dead, and you need to focus on yourself."

"Reading the newspaper isn't a crime," I said.

"They teach you to disrespect your parents in school?" she asked.

"Just a comment."

Her lips curled while she took a longer drag. "Time for another lesson."

"The fuck you talking about?"

"You know I hate it when you curse."

Either Mom was drunk off her ass or she was the biggest fucking hypocrite—she cussed all the time. Mom also never had a problem with me using bad language before.

"I'm gonna go rest before dinner." I threw the newspaper on the counter, then Mom grabbed me with her free hand when I tried leaving the kitchen.

"You'll leave when I'm done with the lesson."

"And what's that?" I asked.

"Lean forward," she spat.

I didn't move. Mom wasn't the boss of me no matter how much she thought she was.

"You know the lesson will be ten times worse if you don't obey me," Mom said.

Fuck. She had a point. So, I followed Mom's instructions despite how my pulse remained audible in my ears. Nothing like fearing the unknown—there was just no telling what Mom would do.

Mom huffed out a sigh. "I want you to know I'm doing this because I love you."

"Doing what?" I asked.

I screamed louder than I ever had before. Mom just pressed her cigarette, which remained lit, against my right cheek.

I could've shoved Mom off me and then slit her throat with one of the kitchen knives. But it didn't matter what the fuck I did. I could go to jail if I killed her. I didn't like to dwell on the issue much—the humiliation was still palpable—but I had gone to the police once, only to not be believed. So, I'd be trading one prison for another. Truthfully, my life was worthless. The only thing worse than having false hope was having no hope at all. In a perfect world, I would've found hope in even the darkest situation. But no. There was no possibility of escaping Mom.

"Better treat me with respect in the future. Next time it'll be the stove." Mom puffed on her cigarette, then extinguished it on the silver ashtray on the kitchen counter. She strutted out of the kitchen—almost as if she was proud of herself.

I waited till I could no longer hear her footsteps before crying. But my sobbing wasn't only because Mom just burned me with a cigarette— my gaze just shifted to the newspaper. More specifically, the front-page headline about the police ruling Declan's death an accident. Bullshit. I couldn't believe Declan would shoot himself with one of his father's guns because he was tipsy.

So, I'd investigate Declan's death myself. I owed it to him to see if there was more to his death. Being proven wrong was the worst thing that could happen, because I had nothing left to lose. That was the perk of leading an empty life.

CHAPTER 5

I entered the kitchen the following morning, discovering my car keys weren't in the ceramic bowl by the fridge.

My heart raced. Something must've been wrong. I always left my car keys in the same spot when coming home from school. That way, I'd know where they were.

Mom cackled after entering the kitchen. "Something wrong?"

"Have you seen my car keys?"

"Yes."

"Great. Where are they?"

"With the new owner of the car."

I blinked. "Come again?"

Her grin expanded, accentuating her yellowish teeth—good to know there was some justice in the world since her years of smoking might've been catching up to her. "I decided to give away your car," she said. "You just missed the person. Wonderful woman."

"You fucking bitch."

She raised her eyebrows. "Did you forget yesterday's lesson?"

"When'd you decide to give away my jeep?" I asked.

"A couple of days ago. Think of it as your punishment for going to Declan's party."

"You said you weren't angry because you didn't witness anything."

"Yes. That's true." She paused for a second. "But you need humbling. So, I'm doing you a favor."

"Only you could frame controlling behavior as kindness."

"You should go. I wouldn't want you missing the bus and having to walk the six or so miles to school."

I screamed at Mom. I couldn't believe she'd take my car from me—that was a new low for her. Robbing me of my transportation was almost worse than burning me with a cigarette. I could only afford an UBER to Declan's party because of both a discount on my first ride and because of leftover money I saved from doing random tutoring gigs last year. So, it wasn't like I could always leave the house if my dynamic with Mom declined further. And I also had no idea when Gina would be available to hang next, so I couldn't count on her.

"I'm not kidding," Mom said. "The bus will come any minute."

I spat in Mom's face without considering the consequences. Any possible retaliation from her didn't matter. Not when I wanted her to feel the visceral humiliation she made me feel on a daily basis. For once, I reversed the dynamic between us. And it felt fucking incredible. Maybe, just maybe, Mom would back off. I didn't care how terrible the idea sounded. Defeating a bully sometimes meant having to be the bigger bully. "Go to Hell!" I exclaimed.

Mom didn't speak. Instead, she rubbed the spit from her face.

"Have a good day," I said.

I walked through the school hallway after getting the notebooks and textbooks for my morning classes, only to bump into someone. My pulse drummed faster in my ears after I looked up at the person. It was Tripp.

I hung my head. "Not trying to start anything. Just got distracted because I wasn't paying attention to where I was going."

"Don't let it happen again." Tripp sighed. "I mean, it's fine."

"Bye," I mumbled.

"Wait," Tripp said.

I cocked my head. "The fuck do you want? You made it clear you didn't want anything to do with me."

"About that…"

"I don't have time for this. Wouldn't want Mr. Hopper to give me detention for being late to math class."

Tripp pulled me to the side. "What the hell happened to your face?"

My stomach tightened. If I didn't invent an excuse fast, then Tripp would discover what happened to me. And I couldn't have that. Confiding in Tripp about my bad home situation wouldn't change my life. It'd still suck.

"Just a little clumsy," I said.

He stared me down. "Really?"

"Calling me a liar?"

"Please don't put words in my mouth," Tripp stammered. "I can't help thinking how that wound looks like a burn mark."

"If you have something to say, then say it."

Tripp stuffed his hands into the pockets of his varsity jacket. "I shouldn't have given you a hard time when you apologized. You made a stupid mistake and deserve an opportunity to change."

The side door opened, blowing a gust of wind through the hallway while a teacher entered the building. A few pieces of paper even fell off the bulletin board.

I snickered. "How kind of you."

Tripp's cheeks flushed. "I'm willing to give you another chance."

"Don't think so."

His Adam's apple bobbed. "Huh?"

"You can't change your mind because you're bored."

Tripp clenched his jaw. "You aren't listening. I'm saying I overreacted."

"Don't care what you call it. I'm done." I walked away from Tripp without another word.

Regret panged through my body while I fought back tears. I didn't want my dynamic with Tripp to be this way. I just wasn't sure how I was supposed to tell Tripp how I was the textbook example of how broken people hurt others. I also couldn't have Mom discovering my sexuality. If she did, then her burning me with a cigarette would seem like Christmas Day compared to what she would've done if she knew I was bisexual.

The bell rang, signaling the end of math class.

I had the unfortunate luck of Tripp sitting next to me, although at least he hadn't bothered chatting with me. No telling how I would've reacted if he got in my face. Discreetly talking to Tripp in the school hallway was one thing, but I refused to let anyone discover the truth about my interactions with him. Only one wrong move and people would discover Tripp and I had slept together.

Mr. Hopper adjusted his glasses when I finished shoving everything into my backpack. "Can we talk, Colton?"

"Okay."

I cursed under my breath, then approached Mr. Hopper's desk. Like Mom, it was better to just let Mr. Hopper say whatever he wanted to say.

"Everything okay?" Mr. Hopper asked.

"Why do you ask?"

"I couldn't help noticing your face."

Deep breaths. He only made an observation, not an accusation. So, I could still spin the situation. I'd have to be more careful in the future, though. If Tripp and Mr. Hopper were suspicious about the burn mark on my face, then other people could be as well. And I couldn't have that. Nosey questions wouldn't help me. They would just increase my aggravation.

"So?" I demanded.

Tripp shuffled out of the classroom, so it was just Mr. Hopper and I to ourselves.

"If something is going on, then I hope you'd consider telling me," Mr. Hopper said.

"Don't you have to report certain shit?"

"I don't always follow the rules. Like when I didn't give you detention the other day."

"Trying to make me feel guilty?" I asked.

"I'm only asking because I care."

Mr. Hopper's good intentions didn't matter. That was the thing about being an abuse victim. Trusting another adult after everything Mom did to me was hard. Mr. Hopper could've been lying about how he wouldn't report this if I told him the truth. Couldn't take the risk. Mom would only make me suffer more if people confronted her with a possible abuse allegation. She'd be furious if social services paid us a visit.

I chuckled. "I'm just clumsy. No big deal."

Mr. Hopper opened his desk drawer before taking out a pad. He scribbled something on the sheet and ripped it off. Then, he handed the paper to me.

"What the fuck is this?" I asked

"A late pass."

I gave him a look. "Okay?"

"In case you wanted to go to the bathroom and take a minute to pull yourself together before your next class."

"Thanks," I forced out.

I left his classroom without another word, finding Tripp standing outside by the door. Almost as if he waited for me. I avoided eye contact, then darted down the hallway without so much as thinking about looking back at Tripp. I couldn't. If I met his gaze or indulged him for a chat, then I might purge my feelings. Hard to deny someone like Tripp if his soft, brown eyes remained focused on me.

CHAPTER 6

I entered my guidance counselor's office the next day during one of my free periods. The door clinked shut behind me, then I sat on the chair in front of Mrs. Duran's desk. She grabbed a hair tie from her desk, ran her fingers through her hair, then placed her hair into a ponytail.

My heart pounded faster. If I wasn't careful, Mrs. Duran might discover the truth about my toxic home life.

Mrs. Duran placed her elbows onto her mahogany desk while she adjusted her posture in her chair. "Must be wondering why I emailed you last night about meeting today."

No shit. She only emailed saying I needed to stop by during fourth period. Nothing else. No hint of me being in trouble. No hint of her praising me about something. I didn't bother filling the silence.

Her face drooped. "I'm sorry about Declan's death. This must be a difficult time for you."

"The fuck you care?"

She bit her lip. "You were supposed to email me the list of colleges you wanted to apply to. But you never did."

I shrugged. "Oops."

"If you're lost about where to start looking, then I can help. But I can't do anything unless you communicate with me."

I snorted. Mrs. Duran was clueless like most other adults. Not sure how I could be honest with her about anything when I couldn't even be honest with myself about wishing my life could be different.

But no. This was the real world, and dreams didn't happen on a whim like in Disney movies.

"I'm not planning on applying to colleges," I blurted.

"Excuse me?"

"I'm not kidding."

"May I ask why?"

"Not like I'd even get into a school." I paused for a beat. "I got all C's during the past three years. And I'm barely passing any of my current classes—I have a D in most of them."

I laughed. I couldn't help being amused by the irony of how I tutored people despite getting C's all throughout high school. That was the thing, though. I wasn't doing poorly in my classes because I didn't understand the material—I did. I just couldn't find the proper motivation.

She sighed. "If there's extenuating circumstances, then I'm sure your teachers would be happy to work with you. Or we could have one of the National Honor Society students tutor you if it's an issue of not understanding the material."

"Nothing matters."

"There's art schools too," Mrs. Duran. "Perhaps that'd interest you, because grades aren't everything to them."

I fought back tears. Her comment was the first time an authority figure said anything remotely supportive to me. It was a shame, really. My life could be different if an adult intervened in my life earlier.

I couldn't swallow the lump in my throat. I had to take a second to mourn for the life I could've had. My only crime was being born to the wrong mother. And there wasn't a fucking thing I could do about it.

"Nope," I said.

She hissed at me. "I'm really trying. But you've gotta meet me halfway."

"Okay…"

"You can be anything you wanna be."

"No, I can't," I said.

She sipped her coffee. "If you don't wanna go to college, then what are your plans for life after school?"

"Be an assistant at my mother's real estate office."

"Perhaps we should change the subject." Mrs. Duran drummed her fingers against her desk. "I can't help noticing your small bruise on the right side of your face."

"So?" I asked.

"Everything okay at home?" she asked.

Sweat clung to my forehead. I hadn't forgotten about my conversation with Mr. Hopper, and I almost accidentally bit my tongue from thinking too hard.

I glared at her. "Why would you ask that?"

"If there's something you wanna share with me, then I promise I won't tell anyone. Not even if it's something I'd have to report."

"Save it."

"Huh?" she asked.

I rolled my eyes. "I've heard this all before. Anyway, I'm done."

I stood, then shuffled towards the door.

"My door is always open in case you wanna chat," Mrs. Duran called out. "Promise not to judge."

I slammed the door shut before scurrying down the hallway. I even passed Tripp, and locked eyes with him before letting go of a breath once he was out of sight. Not having him in my life was best. Not like he could save me from Mom—nobody could.

I sat in the back left row of the church Saturday morning.

The church was only a mile from my house, so I walked to the funeral.

Relief pulsed through my body for a beat. I was glad to see that the church was packed. Declan deserved a proper funeral, because he'd be forgotten soon enough.

I cocked my head, then my throat constricted. I stole a glance with Tripp, who sat a couple of rows ahead of me with the rest of the football team.

The priest approached the podium, then leaned into the microphone.

Tears formed in my eyes, and I didn't suppress them. Not this time. The majority of people were crying or sobbing, so nobody would say anything about me being a pussy for showing emotion.

Declan died, yet I didn't have to forget about him. Not when he was the first person at Lakewood High to ever accept me.

I stood by my locker before first period during the second Friday of freshman year. And I couldn't help being consumed by dread. Even school was preferable than being stuck at home with Mom for two days.

Footsteps squeaked against the floor, then Declan approached me.

He handed me a flier. Hell, he even smiled at me.

I waved the paper at him. "What the fuck is this?"

"I'm having a party tomorrow night, and you should come. I've invited the entire freshman class."

"Whatever."

He placed his hands on his hips. "Got better plans?"

His response was why negative stereotypes about popular kids existed—I didn't owe him anything. Not like the world would end if he had one less person to flaunt his wealth to. I also couldn't imagine fitting in with Declan's crowd, because I'd probably just stand in the corner of some room, sipping my drink while on my iPhone.

I crackled my knuckles. "Not exactly."

Declan pulled me to the empty, adjacent hallway. "There's something else I wanted to chat with you about."

"Okay…"

"You know we're in a lot of the same classes?"

"So?" I demanded.

"I've seen you looking at old issues of *People* in class."

I made a pig-like snort. "The fuck you getting at?"

He stuffed his hands into his pockets. "It's okay if you're gay. Nobody would care if you're into dudes."

Mom might as well have pressed a lit cigarette against my back. Declan couldn't be that perceptive—my world would end if people discovered this secret. And Declan would drop the conversation if he didn't want me to punch him, because that was what I was five seconds away from doing. Declan didn't know me. So, he had no right to speak so frankly to me. As if he wasn't conceited enough.

"You better watch what you say next," I said.

"Absolutely, no judgment. If I were gay, then I'd be drooling over pictures of Channing Tatum too."

My cheeks burned, yet I couldn't respond. Someone knew my deepest secret, and I didn't know what the fuck I would do. Nobody could know I was attracted to guys. Not now. Not ever.

"I'm not trying to embarrass you," Declan said. "I've also noticed how you either always sit by yourself or go to the library during lunch."

"And?"

"There's no reason to be ashamed," Declan said.

"You don't know a fucking thing about me."

"Being you must be exhausting."

Damn. There Declan went making another assumption about my life. He wasn't helping my impression of him. If I was ever gonna be honest and vulnerable with someone—even in a strictly platonic way— then I needed to do it on my own timetable. Not because a classmate felt compelled to talk with me.

"You haven't told me what you fucking want," I said.

"You need a friend, and I'm happy to be one."

I gave him an icy expression, skepticism pulsing through my body. "I'm not some project."

"Never said you were."

"I like girls too."

"So you're bisexual. No big deal."

"It's a big deal to me."

He shook his head. "It shouldn't be. Look, man, I don't mean to sound trite. But you're lucky to be alive, because some people don't have that luxury."

"Come again?"

"My older sister committed suicide when I was eleven. She suffered from an eating disorder for years, and was convinced she'd never be good enough. Hiding from her feelings killed her. Don't be like that."

Regret panged through my body. I never liked Declan, yet even I couldn't help feeling sympathy about his sister. He didn't deserve to deal with a serious issue so early in life. Nobody did. He'd have to live with his sister's death for the rest of his life. I should know. I'd have to live with the pain of my toxic home situation for the rest of my life no matter how much I wished the opposite were true. I couldn't have been more wrong about Declan's understanding of pain.

"Sorry to hear that," I said.

"I'm not gonna tell you how to live your life, but you don't have to be miserable." Declan fixed his backpack strap. "Unless you don't want to be happy."

"Thanks, Dad."

Declan clapped my shoulder. "Hope you come to my party. Would be great to have a new face. Can only tolerate the same company for so long."

Fuck. There was no stopping Declan. He was like a student with a 98 average, pestering their teacher for extra credit because they just couldn't live without a perfect average.

I pressed my hands together, whimpering. "Please don't tell anyone about this conversation. You've got no idea what would happen if the truth came out."

Declan raised his palm. "It'll be our secret."

"Thanks," I whispered.

The priest's coughing snapped me out of my digression.

He remained at the podium, and I had no idea when he'd finish blabbing. Although I was more concerned about someone else. Tripp. I locked eyes with him again, and my heart even fluttered. I just couldn't help feeling weak about Tripp, because I would've given anything for things to be different with him.

I exited the church bathroom sometime later.

I hadn't been in a rush to return home after the service ended. Mom was probably still hungover. So, it wasn't like she'd do anything to me if I didn't return home right away after the funeral.

A gust of wind swooshed into the church after I opened the door. After that, I shuffled onto the sidewalk before walking through the parking lot.

One of only a couple of vehicles left in the church parking lot honked their horn at me. The driver's seat window of the Mercedes rolled down. It was Tripp.

"Need a ride?" he asked.

"Nah. I'm good."

"Sure?"

"You can go," I said.

"Someone picking you up?"

Tripp needed to be careful. If I didn't know better, then I would've thought he cared about me.

"I'm gonna walk home," I said. "My house is only a mile from here."

Rain pattered against the ground.

Tripp beamed his eyes. "Why don't you let me drive you? Not a big deal. Not like I've got anything better to do."

"What about stopping by Declan's house?" I asked.

"The luncheon is only for immediate family."

"Stupid me. Must've forgotten."

"Why don't you let me drive you?" Tripp asked.

"I'm good."

"Why do you always have to be so difficult?"

My mouth gaped. No one had said that to me before. In a perfect world, I wouldn't have accepted Tripp's offer without trying to maintain my façade. I wouldn't die from Tripp driving me home.

Tripp grinned. "My parents are once again away for the weekend."

"Lucky you."

"I don't have to drop you back home if you don't want. You could come back to my house for the afternoon. You'd be doing me a favor, because I could use the company."

My heart almost leapt out of my chest. I shouldn't have entertained Tripp's suggestion, but I couldn't help myself. Declan was right about what he said the first day he met me. Being me was fucking exhausting. So, it'd be nice to take away the pain. Even temporarily.

I flashed a smile. "Sure. That'd be nice."

Tripp snickered. "Great."

I jogged over to the front passenger seat.

Tripp extended his arm, then opened the door like a gentleman.

Tripp and I remained in bed, comforter wrapped around us.

Sweat dripped down both of our faces while we caught our breath. Mercury must've been in retrograde because I couldn't believe I just slept with Tripp. Yet I did. No amount of blinking changed how Tripp was in bed next to me.

"Damn!" Tripp exclaimed.

"Good to know you enjoyed yourself."

Tripp winked. "Hope you had fun too."

"I did."

"Let me know when you're ready to go, and I'll drive you back home," Tripp said. "And it's not a problem if you want me to drop you off a block away from your house."

I didn't know whether to laugh or scream. I hadn't anticipated Tripp wanting to get rid of me within a couple minutes of our hookup.

"Do you want me to leave?" I asked.

"I didn't say that."

"Then what?"

Tripp let out a small laugh. "No offense, but a cactus is more welcoming than you."

"Seriously?"

"I'm kidding."

I maintained our eye contact, then leaned closer. "Maybe I wanna stay and have that late lunch you mentioned."

I couldn't believe what just came out of my mouth. Here I was, prolonging my time with Tripp. Almost as if I wanted to pretend he was my boyfriend.

"You don't owe me anything. I'm fine with this being just sex, so don't feel obligated to share a meal with me," he said.

I chuckled. "Now who's the difficult one?"

"Don't want you to feel obligated to stay."

I caressed his right cheek. "Nobody makes me do anything I don't want to."

"Fair enough."

I remained silent, eyes glued to Tripp. I couldn't get enough of him, because I would've given anything to never have to leave his bed. Something alluring just existed from how someone like me—someone who was callous, harsh, and withdrawn—relinquishing control for a little while and being the submissive one.

Tripp pushed a lock of my hair to the side. "What are you thinking about?"

"I'm still not into guys. You're just fulfilling my physical needs because I haven't hooked up with any girls."

"You can be whoever you wanna be around me," Tripp said.

"Thanks," I forced out.

He squeezed my hand. "I'm serious."

"Good to know someone cares."

"I'm not gonna force you to tell me anything you don't want to, but I can't help thinking about the bruise on your head."

"Tripp, please!"

"If someone—like your mother—is abusing you, then you've gotta speak up. You shouldn't suffer in silence."

"Whatever. Anyway, what were you gonna make?" I asked.

"Fine." Tripp grabbed his tee-shirt from the middle of the bed, then slipped into it in a matter of seconds. "We don't have to discuss your bruise if you don't want to. But know you can vent to me whenever you want to."

"You didn't answer my question."

"Spaghetti Carbonara. That's what I was gonna cook."

I smirked. "I bet you'd look cute in an apron."

He rubbed my nose. "You wish."

CHAPTER 7

I sat on Declan's living room couch several afternoons later. A tray, consisting of two teacups and a plate of cookies, was on the living room table. A woman with her hair wrapped in a bun sat to the left of me, and I soon cocked my head.

I gave her a quick smile. "Thanks for agreeing to meet, Mrs. Price."

"Call me Judy."

"Okay."

"Anyway, no thanks necessary." Judy grabbed a cookie and munched on it. "Nice talking with someone who isn't family."

"I hope you didn't think me reaching out was odd."

She giggled. "Tell me whatever is on your mind. It can't be worse than any of the thoughts I've had since Declan died."

"Something has been bugging me about what happened to Declan."

She raised an eyebrow. "Like what?"

"Declan never struck me as a clumsy guy. Even if he could've been tipsy when he died."

"What are you saying?" Judy asked through gritted teeth.

"Do you agree with how the police ruled his death an accident?"

She shrugged. "I'm not a detective, crime scene technician, or medical examiner."

"I know."

"But I'm glad you mentioned your concern."

Interesting. Good to know I might not have been alone in thinking there could've been more to Declan's death. If someone else thought something similar, then my theory might be true.

I blinked. "You are?"

"I overheard something at Declan's funeral."

"You don't have to tell me if you don't want to." I sipped my tea. The sweet aroma from the honey lingered on my tongue before I swallowed the gulp of tea and licked my lips.

"Venting might be good."

I nodded. "Whatever makes you happy."

"A couple of teenagers were talking about how Declan was dealing drugs."

Dumping a bucket of ice on me would've shocked me less than what Judy said. Discovering Declan might have been dealing drugs was the last thing I expected to happen during my conversation with Judy. Still, I didn't need to be psychic to understand why Judy might've wanted to link the drug dealing to Declan's death. Desperation was a consequence from tragic situations. I should know, after all—there were numerous times that I wanted a concrete reason for why the universe chose me to have an abusive mother. Dying because of a drug deal gone bad was sad, but at least then Judy would've had a specific target for her anger.

"Anything concrete?" I asked.

"Not really."

"That must've been difficult for you to hear," I said.

"I'm not clueless. I was a teenager once, so I've made my fair share of bad choices."

"Do you think dealing is something Declan would do?" I asked.

She pursed her lips. "I don't know. You tell me."

"Huh?"

"You must've known Declan better than I did."

I let out a nervous laugh. "I'm sure that's not true."

She chugged the rest of her tea. "Don't be ridiculous. All teenagers prefer hanging out with their friends over their parents."

"Fair enough."

"Mind if I ask you a question?"

I shook my head.

"Why are you so curious?" Judy continued.

"Intuition."

"That's both a gift and a curse."

She was right; I needed to be careful. I might get an answer I didn't like, and then I'd have to live with the truth.

I took a cookie and devoured it within a couple of seconds. "True."

"It's not like Declan needed the money—he got a monthly allowance." Judy forced in a breath. "Although money isn't everything."

"Pardon me?"

"Teenagers sometimes do bad things because they're bored."

My iPhone buzzed inside my pocket, then I took it out. I had several missed text messages from Mom asking where the fuck I was.

Whatever. Mom couldn't control me every second of the day no matter how much she wished she could. I wasn't a doll; I was a fucking human being.

"Something wrong?" Judy asked.

"No." I drank the rest of my tea, then stood. "Just didn't realize it was this late."

"Sorry. I didn't mean to keep you."

"Don't worry about it."

She blew a loose strand of hair out of the way. "Thanks again for stopping by. Feel free to drop by anytime."

"Will do." I exited the living room without another word despite my sympathy pangs for Judy. Knowing her entire life story wasn't necessary to understand her current emotional state. If she gave me an open invitation to visit her whenever I wanted, then she must've been lonely. Declan and I were friends, but it wasn't like I was his best friend. Not like one of his buddies from the football team. And I wasn't exactly a pillar of the community because of my loser, drunk mother.

I shut the front door, making sure not to slam it. A distinct chill permeated the air while the trees bobbed in the wind.

I couldn't stop thinking about her revelation about Declan possibly being a drug dealer, though. If Declan was dealing, then that could've provided a motive for murder. Maybe a rival dealer shot him. Or maybe it was an angry client. Perhaps the person who shot Declan made it look like an accident. I also wasn't a detective, crime scene technician, or medical examiner, but maybe the angle of the gunshot wound was slightly ambiguous. And in a rich town like Lakewood, it was understandable why the police would prefer Declan's death to be an accident as opposed to murder. Deciding he died while playing with one of his family guns tied up his death in a neat bow.

I continued walking down Declan's driveway, which must've been the longest driveway I ever saw. To hell with how some people might've thought I was neurotic or obsessive for thinking Declan's death was too convenient. I had nothing to lose by playing amateur detective. I owed it to Declan to uncover the truth about his death—whatever that might be.

The wind whipped through the air louder and faster this time, stinging my face. I was gonna have to use almost all my remaining money left to take an UBER home.

Mrs. Duff squealed, snapping me out of my daydreaming. "We're in one of the best parts of the semester. You'll partner up and pick a short story or multiple short stories to do some kind of presentation to the class about writing craft."

I was seated in a row in the back of my creative writing classroom, and I almost groaned. The idea of doing a project made me wanna yank my hair out. I couldn't have anything distract me from my possible lead in Declan's death.

"This might be a project, but I don't want you to feel stressed," Mrs. Duff continued. "The structure is very open-ended."

"Are you gonna pick our partners?" piped up a girl in the front row.

Mrs. Duff snorted. "Don't be silly. That's your job."

Tripp, who was sitting next to me, tilted his head. "Partners?"

I didn't even hesitate. "Sure."

Someone should've given me a medal. I just allowed myself to be vulnerable—the old me would've fretted about growing closer to Tripp. But our hookup from last Saturday remained etched in my mind. Like me on the bed on my stomach while Tripp wrapped an arm around me while we had sex. He could've placed both arms on the bed. Yet he didn't. Almost as if he wanted to feel an emotional connection in addition to a physical connection.

"We can work on it after school today since I don't have football practice," he said. "Unless another day would be better for you."

"Today works," I said.

Tripp winked. "Your house or mine?"

I gave Tripp a dirty look.

Tripp elbowed me. "Kidding."

"No worries."

The bell rang.

"Meet me in the parking lot after eighth period, and I'll drive us home." Tripp beamed his eyes at me. "My parents have a dinner party tonight, so they'll be gone all afternoon and evening."

"Sounds good."

I breathed a sigh of relief while students darted out of the classroom. This is what happiness must've been like, and I loved every fucking minute of it. For once, I was getting something I wanted—more time with Tripp. And I'd enjoy every second with Tripp. It'd only be a matter of time before Mom went ballistic and hit me or burned me with a cigarette.

CHAPTER 8

I approached Warner Jameson in the school hallway after Tripp and I partnered up on the creative writing project.

I forced a smile. "Have a sec?"

Warner rubbed the top of his head, accentuating his buzz cut. "Sure."

I pulled Warner to the side. Students continued flocking through the hallway, and I didn't want anyone to overhear our conversation.

I coughed, clearing the nervousness from my throat. "I'm sorry for your loss. Declan's death must've been the hardest on you—I know you two always did everything together."

"Seriously?"

Warner didn't need to act standoffish. I was easing into the serious conversation like any good amateur detective would've done.

"This is important," I pleaded.

"Get to the point."

"I heard a rumor about Declan, and I was wondering if you could clear up my confusion."

He tugged at the sides of his varsity jacket. "Why me?"

I scrunched my nose. "Being best friends with Declan means you must've known things about him that nobody else did."

"So?"

"I heard he was dealing drugs," I blurted.

Fuck worrying about seeming awkward. I wouldn't get anywhere with Warren if I continued stuttering.

He snorted. "What a load of shit."

"Excuse me?"

Warren stepped closer—so close that his coffee breath almost tickled my skin. "I wanna know where you heard the rumor."

"Doesn't matter."

"Yeah, it does."

"Answer my question," I said.

"He wasn't dealing drugs." Warren paused for a beat, averting his gaze. "And I have no idea why someone would lie about that. Maybe the person was jealous."

Interesting. Warren's idea was reasonable enough. Half the students in the school might've been jealous of Declan because of his family's wealth.

"Perhaps," I said.

"Why would you wanna even ask a question like that?" Warren asked. "Haven't you heard that expression about leaving sleeping dogs alone?"

I remained silent, unsure of what to say.

"Well?" Warren demanded.

I shrugged. "Curiosity isn't a sin."

"It'd be a shame to desecrate Declan's memory. Let him rest in peace."

I didn't respond. Instead, I continued staring at him.

He hissed. "What? Didn't know jocks had a good vocabulary. Well, here's a bombshell. Not every football player is dumb."

"Fair enough."

My pulse drummed louder in my ears. Whether I accepted the truth or not, this conversation wasn't going the way I wanted it to. Getting a piece of information that confirmed my theory about how Declan's death was murder and not an accident was ideal. The universe could've let me get my way for once in my life. Not like I wanted to win the lottery.

"I'm actually glad you wanted to chat," Warren said.

"You are?"

"I heard about your fight with Tripp."

"Huh?"

"Don't play dumb," Warren said. "The whole school knows about your altercation and how Tripp is the only reason your sorry ass didn't get expelled"

I snickered. Using an SAT word like desecrate didn't mean Warren was smart. It just meant he knew one fancy word. If he were smart, then he'd just say whatever he wanted to say.

"What's your point?" I asked.

He sneered. "You better not cause more trouble for Tripp."

"That's none of your fucking business."

"I'm on the football team with Tripp, which makes it my concern." Warren forced a breath.

Warren didn't need to be a jackass. I tried being nice to him with this conversation. But no. The universe had other plans for me like everything else in life. So, bravado was my only option. If I tricked myself into not being afraid, then maybe I wouldn't be afraid. I couldn't forget how Warren was both on the football team and at least half a foot taller than me. So, he could beat me in a fight if this conversation escalated further. I would've even bet my life on it.

"Whatever," I said.

"And don't ask any more stupid questions about Declan's death." He cackled. "If I were you, I'd mind my own fucking business."

Wow. If I didn't know better, then I would've suspected Warren seemed defensive about Declan's death. I hadn't put pressure on the police to reopen Declan's case or gone to the local media with my theory. So, Warren needed to chill. It wasn't the end of his world if I allowed myself to be curious about Declan's death.

I gave Warren a mock frown. "Ouch. I'm so scared."

"Have a good day." Warren smacked his shoulder against mine before shuffling down the hallway. He was soon out of sight, leaving me to my own thoughts.

I tilted my head, locking eyes with Tripp who just walked out of the bathroom at the opposite end of the hallway.

My shoulders shook. Hopefully, Tripp hadn't witnessed my conversation with Warren. We were barely back on speaking terms, and our dynamic couldn't once again end before we explored what we meant to each other.

Tripp darted away. Maybe, just maybe, Tripp's reaction was a good sign. If he saw my conversation with Warren, then he could've stormed over to me and demanded an explanation. But he hadn't, so I'd assume everything was okay with him for the moment.

Tripp and I sat in his bedroom after school, laptop resting on his desk.

He brushed his hand against mine before moving his arm to the keyboard and typing some more. Sweat rolled down my back, and every neuron in my body became electrified—our brief touch was still palpable.

I wanted to scream. Tripp and I hadn't discussed what our hookup the day of Declan's funeral meant, and I didn't know what to do. If I was too aloof, then Tripp might think I didn't care. But if I was too honest, then Tripp might get scared.

However, I couldn't deny one truth. I wanted Tripp. I wanted to run my fingers through his hair, to feel the friction of his smooth hands against my cheeks, to have his tongue in my mouth, and to inhale the scent of whatever deodorant he used.

I had to decide if I was gonna be cautious or take a risk, because I'd never get what I wanted unless I verbalized my feelings to Tripp.

He lifted his gaze from his laptop. "Something wrong?"

"Nah, I'm good."

"Cool." Tripp resumed typing.

"Sorry. I should be contributing more."

He chuckled. "Don't be ridiculous. This project is all you. I'm just typing up what you said."

"I'm not sure about that..."

"You're the one who pointed out how the dialogue in the short story creates a snappy pace, reveals characterization, and contains subtext."

"I guess."

Tripp saved the work, then closed his laptop. "Done."

I blinked. "Really?"

"Yup."

I grabbed my backpack from the floor, then stood. "Can you please drive me home?"

Tripp grabbed my hand. "Wait, Colt!"

I still didn't know how to feel about a nickname. "Colt" seemed like an unusual nickname. Unless the gesture showed I meant something to Tripp.

"Something wrong?" I asked.

"Can we talk?"

I nodded, then sat back in my chair.

"I didn't wanna push you," Tripp continued. "But it's probably best if we're honest with each other."

My blood pulsed through my body faster, my fingers tingling. Perhaps Tripp caved first, and decided he wanted to chat about our "relationship."

"We haven't discussed our tryst the day of Declan's funeral," he said.

"I see."

"I wanted to know how you feel."

I might as well have been buried alive. If I weren't careful, I'd admit that I enjoyed being vulnerable with Tripp. And that possibility terrified me. Dealing with additional hardship wasn't something I wanted or needed.

"Reconnecting with you was nice," Tripp said.

"Yeah."

"We clearly both enjoyed ourselves."

"True."

His gaze narrowed. "That's all you have to say?"

"What do you want from me?" I asked.

He exhaled a breath. "If you won't say it, then I will. I was hoping we could hookup again."

I remained silent. I didn't know what my response should be. I couldn't believe life handed me this gift. Tripp was doing all the work with our dynamic, and I wasn't quite sure how I should feel about Tripp's compassion. Most people wouldn't be so patient.

Having someone like Tripp show genuine interest in me provided more excitement than a child on Christmas morning. Tripp made me feel like a real person. Human nature, really. I challenged anyone not to enjoy someone else wanting them.

Tripp shook his head. "Forget it. The hookup was probably a one-off for you. And that's fine. Not sure why I expected more from you."

My stomach knotted. If I wanted this dynamic with Tripp to last, then I needed to say something. Anything that showed I cared about him. In this moment with Tripp, I wanted to choose happiness.

"You're wrong." I leaned forward, then kissed Tripp.

Fuck it. If there was one thing I learned from English class, then it was the importance of being active and not passive. I'd never be happy unless I pursued my own happiness. So, I'd be vulnerable with Tripp.

Tripp pulled back from the kiss, then grabbed my iPhone, which was on his desk.

"Something wrong?" I asked.

He started typing on my phone. "I never gave you my cellphone number."

"So?"

He returned my iPhone to me. "Never have to use it. Just know my number's there."

Tripp had a point. But not for the reason he mentioned. Having his number would be useful to arrange future hookups, dates, or whatever this was between us.

"Thanks," I mumbled.

"No sweat."

"About the kiss…"

"Would you wanna watch a movie?" Tripp asked.

"Huh?"

"Unless you really need me to drive you home now?"

Perhaps Tripp's offer was about spending more time together in a way that didn't involve pressure. It wasn't like we could have a quickie. No telling when his parents would come home. But not sleeping together this afternoon didn't mean we couldn't enjoy a little more time together before he drove me home. If one of his parents barged in on us, then we could say we were working on a school project.

"A movie sounds great," I replied.

"Any preferences?"

I cracked a smile. "You can pick."

"Cool."

Cawing birds on the tree outside Tripp's bedroom window woke me up.

I yawned and stretched, then opened my eyes. I was in Tripp's bed, but he wasn't next to me.

Wait. Judging from the sunlight sneaking through the bedroom curtains, it must've been morning. As in I spent the whole fucking night at Tripp's place.

Fuck. Mom was gonna wonder where I was.

I grabbed my iPhone, which was plugged into the outlet by the bed. How considerate of Tripp. I certainly didn't remember charging my iPhone.

I turned my iPhone on. I had five text messages from Mom demanding to know where I was.

Fuck. I didn't understand how I'd been so careless with allowing myself to fall asleep in Tripp's bed.

My gaze returned to my phone. I didn't only have several text messages from Mom. I also had a voicemail. Deep breaths, though. No point in getting agitated until I knew what Mom said in her message.

I played the message.

"You've got some nerve thinking you can come and go as you please," Mom said, slurring her words. "You're nothing but an ungrateful piece of shit, and we're gonna have a serious talk when you return from school today. And to think I let attending Declan's funeral slide. What a fucking moron I must be to cut you slack."

I scratched my head. Fuck. I couldn't believe Mom knew I attended Declan's funeral. She had been hungover, so she couldn't have seen me sneak out of the house that day.

I deleted Mom's message, then turned my phone off.

The door opened, revealing Tripp. He locked the door behind him, and my eyes remained glued to him. More specifically, how a towel covered him from the waist down.

Tripp smirked. "Good. You're up."

CHAPTER 9

"The fuck is going on?" I asked.

Tripp chuckled. "You fell asleep while watching the movie, and I didn't wanna wake you. Figured you must've been tired if you dozed off before five."

"Shit." I sat up in Tripp's bed, then glanced at myself—I was still in yesterday's clothes.

"Relax." Tripp walked to his dresser, then pulled out a plaid, button down long-sleeve shirt, tee-shirt, boxers and jeans. "Not like my parents saw you."

Tripp had to have been joking. Easy for him to suggest I relax. His mother wasn't a drunk. There was no telling what Mom would do when I returned home from school later in the day. Her punishment would be worse than burning my cheek with a cigarette. Knowing Mom, she'd follow through with her promise about pressing my face to the stove while it was on.

Tripp removed his towel, then tossed it on the dresser.

"What the hell?" I said, putting my hand in front of my eyes.

"Nothing you haven't seen before, so you might as well enjoy the show."

"Your parents really didn't see me?" I asked.

"Just said a friend needed to crash, and they didn't press the matter."

"Lucky you." My shoulders quaked. I wondered how nice it would be to have parents that didn't ask nosey questions, because I would've killed to be in his position.

"You need to relax." Tripp slid into his boxers, then slipped into his jeans. "My parents already left for work."

"Really?"

Tripp put his tee-shirt on before his long-sleeve button down plaid shirt. "Yup."

"You should've woken me up."

"I was trying to be considerate."

"Doesn't matter," I stammered.

He crossed his arms. "I'm sure your mother won't be angry. And if she is relentless, then work the school project angle."

"It's my fault. I should've been more responsible." I paused for a moment. "I'm so sorry for falling asleep in your bed."

"Don't apologize."

I whipped my head back and forth. "I'm so fucking stupid. It's no wonder why I'm the biggest loser at Lakewood High."

Tripp approached me, then cupped my chin. "I like you."

"You're only saying that because you wanna sleep with me again."

"Not true." He gave me a quick kiss on the lips. "I was thinking we could stop at VERONICA'S, and grab breakfast to go. It's on the way to school."

I could have gotten angry with Tripp wanting to grab breakfast—I could've argued how that showed Tripp was getting too attached to me. But I wouldn't. I couldn't. This warm feeling buzzing through my body felt good. Somehow, Tripp made me forget about my shitty home life. And his "superpower" was worth everything. In this moment, I wanted to choose love and not emotional distance or violence.

"Nothing happened last night?" I asked.

"No. You just fell asleep in my bed," Tripp said. "About breakfast..."

"I'd love to, but I'm low on money."

"My treat."

My hands fell to my lap. "You don't have to pay for my breakfast because you wanna sleep with me again."

He snickered. "I'm not. It's called good karma."

I grabbed a pillow on the bed, then gave him a playful smack with it. "Good to know where your priorities are."

Tripp grabbed the end of the pillow. "Paying for a latte and pastry isn't a big deal."

"If you say so," I said.

Tripp peeked at his alarm o'clock on the table next to his bed, then glanced at me. "We should go if we don't wanna be late."

A good six or so hours passed since I arrived home from school, yet I remained in bed.

Doing nothing proved best, because I needed a strategy. Mom might not have returned yet, but she would eventually. And if I wasn't careful, then we'd have another altercation. And I couldn't have that. I hadn't gotten over how Tripp, Mr. Hopper, and Mrs. Duran pretty much guessed my home situation.

The front door slammed shut, and chills crawled up my spine. Fuck. I was gonna have to deal with Mom whether I wanted to or not.

"Where are you, boy?" Mom asked, screaming in the loudest tone she ever used before. "Time for you to learn another lesson."

I didn't utter a sound. Instead, I covered my hand with my mouth. No harm in making Mom struggle with finding what part of the house I was at. If I could delay a beating or burning by a minute or two, then that was good. Perhaps Mom was so intoxicated that she'd trip and crack her head open on the floor or stairs. Even her falling asleep would've been better than nothing. Then, that would've provided a reprieve.

"I'm serious, boy!" Mom exclaimed. "You better stop acting like a fucking coward and face me."

I didn't speak.

"Perhaps you're in your bedroom," Mom bellowed. "Yeah. That's where I'd hide if I was being a weak little bitch."

Footsteps trudged up the stairs, getting louder with each passing second. Fuck. Mom was gonna find me, and there wasn't a fucking thing I could do about it. I couldn't exactly sneak out my bedroom window—it was on the second floor. And I didn't have anything I could use as a weapon for self-defense. I also couldn't lock my bedroom door—Mom removed the lock years ago. Some shit about how locking my bedroom interfered with her ability to be a good mother.

"This is your last chance." The stairs creaked before Mom made a loud thud when she stepped onto the second floor. "If you surrender now, then I promise I'll go easy on you. Perhaps I'll only burn you with a cigarette for five seconds."

What a fucking monster. My mother was supposed to love me unconditionally, yet she thrived on her demented parenting style the way kids gravitated towards candy and other sweets.

The shuffling of footsteps continued growing louder. Fuck. This was it. Only a matter of seconds before Mom entered my bedroom.

Tears dotted my eyes. I had one tiny truth to hold onto, and that comforted me for a fleeting moment. If Mom killed me tonight, then at least I'd die knowing Tripp and I were honest with each other. I allowed myself to feel something by initiating the kiss in Tripp's bedroom yesterday. Even if vacillating about my true feelings would've been easier. So, I wasn't a total coward.

The door opened. It was Mom.

"Did you miss me?" Mom asked.

I recoiled against my bedroom wall.

"I asked you a question, boy!" Mom slurred.

"How much have you had to drink?" I snapped, giving her a dirty look.

"I'm the parent, not you. So, I'll ask the questions."

"Whatever."

Mom shrilled. "I wanna know why you didn't come home yesterday, and why the fuck you went to Declan's funeral. It's like you actually enjoy these lessons. Unless you know you're so depraved that you need them."

My turn for screaming. "I don't owe you a fucking thing."

"I've had enough of your disrespect." Mom ran to my bed, then yanked me forward in one, swift motion. She threw me against the floor and punched me.

Mom wasn't burning me with the cigarette. That was something, at least.

The punching continued. I wanted to scream but I couldn't find the urge to react. Perhaps Mom finally succeeded with silencing me.

"I don't enjoy this. Just doing this for your own good. With enough of these lessons, you might become a real man, not this faggot version of yourself." Mom continued hitting me, becoming rougher and faster.

Fuck. Maybe this was how my life was gonna end, me on the bedroom floor being beaten to a pulp by my mother.

No. My life wasn't gonna end today. Tripp and the excitement and happiness that dynamic brought me was a reason to live for. So. I was gonna do something I almost never did when dealing with my mother. Fight back.

I summoned all the energy I had before leaning forward and smacked my head against Mom's. Then, I stood.

I wasn't done, though. I kicked Mom several times in the stomach.

"That's for ruining my life, you fucking piece of shit!" I roared. "Do me a favor and go drink yourself to death. Your dying would be the best thing that ever happened to me."

"You'll pay for this," Mom whimpered.

I ran down the hallway and descended the stairs in a matter of seconds, pulse ringing in my ears. I did it. I bought myself a few extra moments while I figured out what I was gonna do. No fucking way was I gonna stay in my house this evening.

I scurried into the kitchen and grabbed the keys from the bowl. There was only one person I wanted to be with. I might not have had my car, but I could steal Mom's car and drive to Tripp's house. Doing the world a favor, really. No telling if Mom would drive drunk later in the evening. Taking Mom's car was also payback for how she stole my car. Wow. Yet another reminder of what a fucking bitch she was.

I hurried out of the kitchen, but my pulse spiked. Mom was at the bottom of the stairs. Fuck. I should've paid more attention to my Greek mythology unit in English class last year. Like when a person chopped off the head of a monster, ten more grew back.

"Where the fuck do you think you're going?" Mom asked, still catching her breath.

"Getting the fuck away from you."

I didn't waste time waiting for a response and ran out the front door. Mom charged after me and caught up to me when I was on the grass. She grabbed my arm. Fuck. This couldn't be it. I was so close to escaping her.

I whirled around, then punched her in the face with all the energy I had. Mom fell backwards onto the grass, screaming.

Mom coughed. "I'm really gonna kill you now, you fucking piece of shit!"

I rushed to the driveway, opened the car, hopped in, and did my seatbelt before barreling out of the driveway. Soon my breathing slowed. Wow. I was gonna have to be more appreciative of the universe. I almost died tonight, and that wasn't a fact I'd forget anytime soon.

I rang the doorbell after stepping onto Tripp's front door.

I paced back and forth on his front porch while my teeth chattered. It was cold enough that I could see my breath. No surprise there—less than two weeks till Halloween.

The door opened. It was Tripp.

I cried before I realized what I was doing. I couldn't contain my feelings anymore. Like with how Mom fucked me up so bad I wondered how trusting Tripp was even possible. Or how it was a miracle I hadn't committed suicide because of my shitty home situation. Or even how I hadn't snapped and killed Mom.

Tripp looked me over. "Everything okay?"

I sobbed louder this time. "I'm sorry to bother you, but I didn't have anywhere else to go."

"No problem."

"Your parents aren't home, are they?"

"Nope," he said.

"I wish it'd stop." More tears fell down my face while the continued chattering of my teeth echoed. I rubbed my hands together, creating friction.

"Don't want you to catch a cold." Tripp walked over to me, then stood behind me before taking his long-sleeve, button down plaid shirt off, and putting it on me. He ushered me inside, then locked the front door.

Tripp led me into the kitchen and gesticulated to the stool on the left. I obeyed his command and sat.

"Don't mean to burden you," I said.

"No big deal."

"I'm sure you must have better things to do then talk to me." I grabbed the left side of Tripp's shirt, which I was still wearing, then sniffed it. The earthly and sweet scent hugged my nostrils. "I'm such a terrible person, and you shouldn't want anything to do with me. I can't even commit to a real relationship."

"None of that matters right now." Tripp opened the freezer, grabbed an ice pack, then tossed it to me. "For the bloody lip."

"Good thinking."

"Have you eaten dinner yet?"

"Excuse me?"

Tripp pointed to the pizza box on the kitchen counter. "Literally just arrived a couple of minutes before you got here. You're welcome to have some. I'd just forget about the leftovers, so you'd be doing me a favor."

"I'd love some pizza."

He laughed. "Good. Thanks for not fighting me."

I belched sometime later. "I'm stuffed. And sorry about burping."

"No worries. My grandma used to say burping was a sign of a successful meal." Tripp snatched a napkin from the kitchen counter, then wiped my lip. "You had a little something."

"Sorry. I'm so clumsy sometimes."

"Stop apologizing." He tossed the napkin in the trash, then caressed my forehead with his free hand. "You're perfect the way you are."

"Doubtful."

Tripp pulled his arm away and cracked his knuckles. "Didn't wanna pressure you at first, but we should talk."

"Okay."

Tripp reached for my hands while maintaining eye contact. "I don't presume to know anything, but you appeared on my doorstep with a bloody lip. And you previously had that bruise on the right side of your face."

My chest expanded and contracted; my breathing became labored with each subsequent breath. I couldn't have been about to tell Tripp everything. Doing so would've been more vulnerable than being the one to kiss him first yesterday. Yet I didn't have a choice. Interrupting Tripp's life meant he deserved an adequate explanation. It was only fair for him to know how fucked up my life was.

His hands remained around mine. "I promise not to judge, so please let me be there for you. It'll only get worse if you bottle up your emotions."

Tripp was right. I was also tired of being a wimp. Telling Tripp about my mom wasn't the cure, but it was a first step.

"You're right," I said, nodding. "There's something seriously fucked up about my life that nobody knows."

Tripp nodded at me.

"My mother physically abuses me, and I can't take it anymore," I said.

He clapped his hand over his mouth. "I'm so sorry, Colt."

The tears returned to my eyes. Best to purge all my feelings. Tripp's kitchen was a safe space, and this conversation was my chance to ask for help.

"But I should start at the beginning when my father abandoned my mother," I said.

CHAPTER 10

"I'm sorry for everything you've been through," Tripp said.

Tripp and I laid in his bed a couple of hours after we finished the pizza. And the bed comforter remained wrapped around us while his mouth gaped. Although no sweat dripped down our faces and our breathing hadn't increased. We hadn't slept together. Not tonight. We really were just talking before bed.

I huffed out a sigh. "What happened to me isn't your fault."

"Doesn't matter. What kind of man abandons his wife and three-year-old son?" Tripp's shoulders tensed. "Only a coward would do that."

"I hope it's okay we didn't have sex tonight."

He scooted closer, then tucked a lock of my hair out of the way. "Don't worry about it. I'd much rather be chatting."

I chuckled. "Good to know."

"I've got one question if you don't mind."

I wish he'd stop trying to sound so formal. Seeing each other naked meant the boundaries between us were virtually nonexistent. He couldn't do anything worse to me than Mom had. Nobody could.

"Sure. Go ahead," I said.

"Have you ever thought about reporting the abuse? It's not the 1950s anymore."

I averted my gaze. "If only it were that simple."

"What are you talking about?" he asked.

"I went to the police a couple of weeks before junior year." I sucked in a breath, closing my eyes for a beat. I never told anyone what I was about to reveal to Tripp.

Tripp squeezed my hand. "We don't have to discuss this if the topic is too painful."

"I filled out a report, and the Lakewood Sheriff even chatted with me." Tears dripped down my face. "He said I was mistaken, and that there was no way my mother could be abusing me. Then, he threw my report in the garbage."

Tripp gasped. "Fuck."

"Sheriff Down is such a fucking piece of shit." I made a fist, then almost screamed. "Sorry. I know violence isn't the answer. The situation was just so unfair—I just wanted someone, anyone to believe me."

Tripp looped his arms around my shoulders, then made eye contact. "I believe you."

"Thanks," I forced out.

"I'm serious."

"I deserve a chance at a good life like everyone else." I sobbed louder and collapsed into Tripp's chest. He hugged me while I did something all too familiar. I closed my eyes. Apparently, I'd be forever grieving the life I'd never have.

We detached from the embrace a couple of minutes later.

"Sorry for getting emotional," I said.

"Don't apologize. Better to let this stuff out than keep it inside," Tripp said. "Although there's something I don't understand."

I raised my eyebrows. "And what's that?"

"Why is your mother so homophobic?"

I shrugged. "I don't know."

My response was truthful. I probably wouldn't get a reason for Mom's hate regardless of how much I wanted one. And that was fine. Nothing Mom said would change my opinion of her. Mom was the scum of the Earth. And Mom's mistakes were so deep that death was the only way to deal with her.

"There's something you should know, Colt."

"Okay."

"My bedroom is a safe space. You can be whoever you wanna be here."

My throat burned. Tripp's response meant more than he'd ever know. He was the first person I could be honest with. And it felt great. For a brief instant, I didn't have to put on a façade.

Damn. If only Tripp came into my life earlier. Maybe, just maybe, my life wouldn't have been so fucked up.

"Great," I mumbled.

Tripp frowned. "I'm not kidding."

"My mother is gonna kill me when I return home," I said. "She'll never forgive me for taking the car."

"Let that be tomorrow's problem."

"I should go home. Better to get it over with."

"Don't talk like that," Tripp said.

"It's the truth. I don't have anything to live for," I said. "I'm not even applying to colleges."

His gaze widened. "If money is an issue, then I can pay. My family has more money than they know what to do with, and I'm sure my parents would be happy to help. They're actually pretty easy-going people compared to most parents."

Offering to pay for my college was the most generous thing anyone ever did for me. Yet the gesture didn't matter. I needed to get into college in order for someone to pay for my education. And that wouldn't happen. I'd be lucky to graduate because of how I was barely passing my classes.

"I'm not worth it," I said.

"You are too," Tripp said.

"I know what most people see when they look at me, and I don't blame them."

Tripp remained silent.

"I'm not stupid. Anyone can see how scary I am," I said. "I just wish more people could see how I'm really just a scared little boy who wants to be loved unconditionally."

Tripp yawned. "I don't mean to be rude, but I'm seconds away from falling asleep. Although I promise we can discuss everything in the morning."

Yeah. No point in getting angry with Tripp because he wanted to cut this conversation short. He listened to me enough as it was. I also didn't have to sleep at my house tonight. So, that was something to be thankful for.

I nodded. "Cool."

"You aren't alone in this." Tripp clapped my shoulder, then moved over to the opposite end of the bed. He turned out the light.

I adjusted my posture, so my back now faced Tripp's side of the bed. Tripp moved back to me before embracing me. He hugged me tighter, then his lips grazed my ear.

"I'll never let anything happen to you," he said.

Tripp's sentiment was nice, but he shouldn't have made promises he couldn't keep. Tripp couldn't be with me every second of the day — I'd eventually have to deal with Mom again.

Sunlight poked through the bedroom curtains the next morning.

I opened my eyes, then stretched. I took my iPhone off the charger and turned it on.

Fuck. I had one new voicemail. It was from Mom.

I played the message.

"If you don't return my car and keys before you go to school, then I'm gonna have your fucking faggot ass arrested," Mom said. "Don't think I won't do it. You're nothing but an ungrateful piece of shit. So, you should be thanking me. You're lucky I haven't kicked you out of the house."

I deleted the message, then turned my iPhone off.

The bedroom door opened, revealing Tripp. A towel remained wrapped around his waist. Although I was more concerned with his smile. His expression was so pure and innocent. Good to know something beautiful still existed in this world.

"What's wrong?" he asked.

"My mother called," I revealed. "I've gotta return her car before first period. Trust me. Avoiding her isn't an option."

"I'll go with you."

"You don't have to do that."

"But I want to," Tripp said. "You can drive her car back to your house, and I'll follow in mine. Then, I'll drive us to school."

"Tripp, please…"

He crossed his arms. "This isn't up for debate, Colt. I'm not gonna let you push me away because you're embarrassed about being vulnerable last night."

Perhaps Tripp had a future as a psychologist—there was no fooling him. But maybe that was a good thing. Whether I accepted the fact or not, I needed someone in my life who'd support me unconditionally.

I walked into the house less than half an hour later.

Mom was sitting on the living room couch, and there was an open bottle of Beefeater gin and glass on the living room table.

Deep breaths. The sooner I returned Mom's keys, the sooner I could go to school and escape her for the next six to seven hours.

She glared at me. "Where the fuck have you been?"

"None of your fucking business."

Mom grunted. "Don't talk to me like that. I'm still your mother."

"Then maybe you should start acting like one."

"You better watch yourself."

I threw the keys at her. But she didn't catch them in time, so they fell onto the floor. No surprise, though. She might've been able to form coherent sentences, although her senses must've already been dulled. Safe to bet that the gin in her glass wasn't her first drink of the day.

"Don't throw stuff at me," Mom continued.

"What are you gonna do about it?" I asked.

Anger pulsed through my body, giving me a brief euphoria. Being confrontational with a nasty woman like my mother might've seemed foolish. But for once, I didn't care what Mom would do to me. I wanted to do something, anything that showed I wasn't some scared kid.

"Maybe burn you with another cigarette. It's what you deserve after running away last night." Mom cracked her knuckles. "Or maybe I'll drown you in the toilet. That'd save me a lot of worry."

An icy feeling crawled up my back. Perhaps it was a mistake to have Tripp stay in his car. Having backup with Mom might've been useful. Yet I couldn't deny how embarrassed I would've been if Tripp witnessed how shitty my home life was. I didn't need him to feel worse for me then he already did.

"You might wanna pace yourself with the drinking." I forced a laugh. "I wouldn't want you to get alcohol poisoning."

"Such an ungrateful piece of shit. If only I went through with my abortion."

I leaned closer to Mom. So close that my breath might have prickled her skin. "I'd be very careful if I were you. Like I mentioned before, I'm not afraid of you."

"We'll see about that." Mom stood in one, quick, swift motion. She tackled me and pinned me against the wall. One hand restrained me to the wall while the other continued gripping my neck.

Damn. Perhaps Mom wasn't as drunk as I thought she was. If she were, then she wouldn't have been able to restrain me.

"I should kill you right here and right now." Mom's hold around my neck intensified. "I could say it was self-defense. Maybe I confronted you about your drinking, and you got violent. I'm sure the police would believe me."

Pouting would've been appropriate if I wasn't on the verge of being strangled. Mom was more demented than I ever imagined. A "normal" parent wouldn't have lied to the police about her son. That was the type of thing that should've only happened in movies and television shows.

The front door opened—it was Tripp. He hurried towards us, then yanked Mom off me before pushing her against the wall.

I caught my breath while the drumming in my ears decreased. Thank goodness Tripp hadn't followed my advice. No telling how much longer I would've lasted if Tripp hadn't ended the altercation between Mom and me.

Tripp spat in Mom's face. "I hope you know what a terrible fucking person you are. Colt doesn't deserve to be treated so shitty."

"Who are you? His boyfriend?" Mom asked.

Boyfriend. I couldn't deny how the word appealed to me, because the label meant I didn't have to go through life alone.

"I don't need to be dating Colt to understand how cruel you are." Tripp released Mom before shoving her against the ground.

"You're lucky I don't call the cops on you," Mom said, remaining on the floor.

"Go ahead," Tripp said.

Relief shot through my body for a moment. Tripp matched Mom blow for blow. Good to know someone wasn't afraid of her. My façade was destined to crumble at some point because I could only be brave for so long.

"Trespassing is a crime," Mom said.

Tripp continued towering over Mom. "So is child abuse."

Mom got up. "Excuse me?"

"I know everything—from burning Colt with cigarettes, to hitting and shoving him, and the emotional abuse too," Tripp said.

"I don't care what you think of me," Mom said.

Tripp tugged at the sides of his varsity jacket. "You should."

Mom tucked a lock of hair behind her ear. "And why is that?"

"I'm not afraid of you." Tripp lunged closer to Mom. "And I'm gonna be checking on Colt regularly."

Mom rolled her eyes. "Your point being?"

"If you don't knock it off with the abuse, then I'll fucking kill you myself. Because that's what someone like you deserves—I bet nobody's ever stood up or threatened you before." His grin expanded. "And I'd get away with it. Being rich means my parents can afford the best attorneys—the kind of lawyers that'd get a jury to feel sorry for me and not care about killing a piece of shit like you."

Relief filled my insides. Normally, Tripp was compassionate, chill, and quick witted. Yet he was so extreme in his comment to Mom.

I didn't care if he'd actually kill Mom or if he was bluffing, though. Someone defended me, and it felt great. Like I was important. I mattered.

Tripp was also absolutely right about his comment. Someone needed to stand up and threaten Mom. Her current quivering lips kinda hinted that death might be the one thing that she feared.

"You talk a good game. I'll give you that," Mom said.

Funny how Mom couldn't invent a better response to Tripp's comment. Almost as if Tripp agitated her more than she realized.

"I'm not kidding," Tripp said. "And I want you to apologize to Colt."

Mom blinked. "Come again?"

Tripp grabbed the bottle of gin from the living room table, then emptied it onto the floor. "I'm serious. If you don't tell Colt that you're sorry, then having an empty bottle of booze is gonna be the least of your problems."

Making Mom express contrition wasn't an exercise in futility. Tripp knew what he was doing. Perhaps it didn't matter if Mom's words were empty. The genius was in the details. Like with how forcing her to apologize would humiliate Mom. And that was worth more than passing grades in all my classes. For once, Mom couldn't get her way by terrorizing me.

Mom jabbed her fist through the air. "How dare you."

Tripp waved the Beefeater bottle at Mom. "Or maybe I'll smack you with this, and end things once and for all."

Mom cocked her head at me. "Sorry for mistreating you. I've been stressed with work, but I promise to do better in the future."

Tripp snickered. "Not good enough."

I loved how he wasn't backing down with Mom. Scrutinizing her apology was what she needed. Mom knew what my life was like now with how she harassed me over every little thing.

"Are you fucking kidding me?" Mom asked.

"Try again. Only this time, show genuine remorse," Tripp said.

Mom exhaled a breath. "I'm sorry for being a bitch, Colton. Won't happen again."

"Better," Tripp said. "Anyway, I'm taking Colt to school now. But have fun waiting for the liquor stores to open."

Tripp grabbed my back, then ushered me towards the front door.

"Funny how you keep referring to my son as 'Colt'." Mom called out.

Tripp and I turned back towards Mom right when we approached the front door.

"What's your point?" Tripp asked.

"Having a nickname for Colton alludes to how you two might be dating," Mom said. "Although I can't imagine what anyone would see in my son."

Fear didn't trickle through my body from how Mom was closer to the truth than she realized. And my reaction wasn't because of how I was too dead on the inside to care about how I should've felt. Mom's words were empty. She didn't have any concrete proof that Tripp and I were together. So, she couldn't do anything to me about Tripp. Especially if Tripp was serious about keeping an eye on Mom and not hesitating with causing trouble for her if she made my life miserable.

Tripp shook his head. "Anyone would be lucky to date him. Colt has a lot to offer, and it's a shame you can't see that."

Tripp started his car a couple of minutes later. We had just put our seatbelts on, and the clunky sound of his ignition echoed. He pulled out of my driveway and drove down the street while my face remained pressed against the window.

Tripp didn't force a conversation after what we went through with Mom. My worst fear came true with Tripp observing how fucked up my home life was, and I didn't know what to do about my current embarrassment. I couldn't go back in time and undo the events of this morning no matter how much I wanted to.

I shifted my gaze to Tripp. If he could try by helping me with Mom, then I wouldn't give him the silent treatment.

"I know no thanks is necessary, but thanks for standing up to my mother," I said, fighting back tears. I couldn't have an emotional breakdown on the way to school. I didn't need my face to be red and my eyes to be puffy during first period. "Nobody has ever done that for me before."

"Figured." Tripp turned left before driving down a new street. "But no thanks necessary. I didn't mean to overstep. Just had a bad feeling when you were taking so long."

"I wouldn't blame you if you wanted nothing to do with me."

"Stop it!" Tripp exclaimed.

"I'm serious. I've got nothing to offer anyone."

"That's not true, and you know it." Tripp honked his horn, and a deer darted into the bushes.

"Whatever," I murmured.

Tripp took one hand off the steering wheel, then patted my knee. "You aren't alone. So never forget that."

"Thanks."

Tripp deserved more than one-word responses, yet I couldn't help myself. I didn't know what I was supposed to do with all these feelings and emotions racing through my mind. Like with how I now had someone in my life who would care if I lived or died.

Gina placed the mugs on our table in the back of VERONICA'S the following afternoon. She then sat in the chair across from me, still flashing a smile.

"Thank goodness you returned my text," Gina said.

"No need to be dramatic."

"It's not dramatic if it's the truth."

"I would've responded eventually."

She giggled. "Yeah. Okay."

I placed my lips on the whipped cream, which was drizzled in caramel, then devoured it. "You didn't have to pay for my latte."

"So?" She twirled a strand of hair around her finger. "Not a big deal."

"You treated last time."

"The outing was my idea."

"What's new with you?" I asked.

"Nice try."

"Excuse me?" I sipped my latte.

"We aren't here to discuss me," she said. "I'm more concerned about you. Like with how you're dealing with Declan's death and your dynamic with Tripp."

I let out a nervous laugh. "Not important."

Gina leaned closer, sliding her elbows onto the table. "I'm not gonna let you slip through the cracks."

"You've been watching too much Dateline."

"This isn't funny, Colton." She drummed her fingers against the table. "I don't expect you to tell me everything, but it'd be nice if you let me in a little."

I looked at the ground. "A part of me still doesn't believe Declan is dead. As for Tripp, we patched things up."

She squealed. "Fantastic. I had no doubt things would work out for you."

Sometimes I wish Gina would dial back her optimism. I'd never be able to understand how a person could be so happy. That was like saying oil and water were the perfect combination.

I wrinkled my nose. "Better not be getting ideas about planning an engagement party for Tripp and I."

"You wish."

I hissed. "I'm serious, Gina."

"You deserve to be happy."

I wouldn't argue with Gina, yet I almost chastised her for her comment. Wanting the best for me was one thing. But I didn't know how I was supposed to be happy. And I wasn't trying to be difficult. Having Tripp and Gina was better than nothing, but my life would never be okay until I didn't have to deal with Mom anymore.

I grabbed a napkin from the metal dispenser, then shredded it into dozens of pieces. "Sure. Whatever."

"What's it like with Tripp?" she asked.

"Not like he's my boyfriend. We're just sleeping together."

Gina chugged the rest of her latte. "Don't do that."

"Huh?"

"Embrace the vulnerability. And you better not think about pushing Tripp away because you're uncomfortable with your feelings."

Wow. Perhaps Tripp wasn't the only one destined for a career in psychology. Seeing through me didn't require much effort for Gina, and I was impressed. The average person wasn't smart enough to be that observant.

I bit my lip. As much I hated admitting the truth, Gina was right. I couldn't risk alienating Tripp. He was the one good thing in my life, and I didn't know what I'd do if I or anything else ruined our dynamic. I was already on my second chance with Tripp, and I'd doubt I'd get a third chance.

I gave her a mock scowl. "Okay, Mom. Anyway, it's your turn to share. You can't tell me you aren't stressed about college applications?"

Having a friend who cared was great, but Gina wouldn't get away with being evasive. The spotlight couldn't be on me all the time.

Gina sucked on her teeth. "Well…"

"Tell me everything. You listened to me, so it's my turn."

"Fine."

"That's more like it."

She picked her nail. "But I don't know where to start. I just can't narrow down the list of colleges I wanna apply to."

"Why don't you tell me the schools you're considering?"

"Really? That might take all week."

My personality officially rubbed off on Gina. It couldn't have taken that long to tell me all the schools she was interested in. So, yeah. She must've exaggerated her comment—I was sure of it.

My eyebrows knitted together. "How many schools are you looking at?"

"Almost twenty," Gina mumbled.

"Then you better start talking."

"Okay."

Whether Gina realized the truth or not, she was being a good friend by discussing her life. This conversation was what I needed—worrying about college applications was a typical teen thing. And I needed more "normal" moments. Wondering about how drunk and abusive Mom would get each evening was no way to live life.

CHAPTER 11

"There's something I wanted to ask you." Tripp turned right before driving down a new road.

"And what's that?" I asked.

"Would you wanna go away for the weekend?" Tripp asked. "My family owns a beach house in Spiderwood."

Spiderwood was a town several hours outside of Lakewood. In fact, a lot of rich people owned a second home there. It was comparable to the Hamptons. My heart even fluttered from Tripp's suggestion. Great to know Tripp cared enough to spend a whole weekend with me.

"What brought this on?" I asked.

"Just thought you might want a getaway." He exhaled a long breath. "Look. I'm not clueless. Threatening your mother the other day was only a temporary solution at best."

I couldn't blame Tripp for his response while my eyes remained glued to the window. I would've been an idiot if I thought Mom would never hassle me again.

"I'm not trying to put pressure on you," Tripp continued.

"I know."

"You don't have to give me a response this second." He remained silent for a beat. "Maybe asking you a loaded question on the way to school wasn't a good idea."

Maybe Tripp spent too much time with me. Backtracking on a statement was the type of thing I would've done.

"I'm not mad," I said.

"You aren't?"

"If I can bully my mother into not caring about my weekend plans, then I'm in."

I was really gonna inform Mom I was going away for the weekend, and there wasn't a damn thing she could do about said fact. The conversation wouldn't be a big deal—I shouldn't have sold myself short. I might've been more capable of defending myself than I realized. I also deserved to have fun, because some clichés—such as only being young once—were true. I only got one chance to be a teen. It wasn't like I could go back in time several years from now when the regret over what could've happened finally hit me.

"Great," Tripp said.

"What about your parents?" I asked. "They won't care about you being away for the weekend?"

"Nope." Tripp halted at a STOP sign. "They're going on a business trip. But they'd be glad the place is getting some use."

"Cool."

"Another thing," Tripp said. "Hopefully, I didn't overstep by offering to drive you to school. That's the last thing I'd want."

"It's sweet."

"It's shameful your mother sold your car."

"You better not buy me a car," I said.

My comment wasn't odd. Tripp offered to have his family pay for my college education. So, there was no telling what other generosity he was capable of. And I'd never admit this, but a small part of me was flattered. Mattering to someone gave me brief joy. So, maybe, just maybe, someone would miss me if I died. The idea of nobody showing up to my funeral was too depressing—even for me.

He chuckled. "I just might."

"Whatever."

"There's one more thing I wanted to know from our conversation the other evening."

"Okay."

"You've never thought about tracking your father down?"

"Don't see the point."

"You don't think it's possible your mother is lying, and that there's more to the story?" he asked.

"I wouldn't be surprised." My chest expanded and contracted several times while my breathing became labored for a moment. It didn't matter how much time passed since my father walked out on me. Dwelling about him was never fun. Feeling as if I was an unwanted child cut me deeper than any knife could've injured me. Parents were supposed to love their child, not treat their child like an afterthought.

I returned home from school hours later. Mom sat on the living room couch, drinking some gin.

I put my backpack on the table by the front door, then strutted into the living room. There was no stopping me. What I was gonna tell Mom had nothing to do with asking her permission. I was going to tell her that Tripp and I were going to Spiderwood for the weekend like it was as natural as breathing.

And no. Mentioning I was going away with Tripp for the weekend wouldn't reveal my sexuality. I could make up some bullshit about how we had a school project we needed to work on and didn't wanna deal with any distractions. Or I could say Tripp was dealing with a personal crisis and asked me to keep him company. The point was, I wasn't afraid to lie. Not when deception meant happiness. I just wouldn't let Mom ruin my connection with Tripp. Mom had already stolen enough from me.

She lifted her gaze off her glass. "Home already?"

"Yup."

"Get out of my sight. I don't even wanna deal with you."

"We've gotta talk."

Mom sipped more gin, then almost choked. "Make it fast."

"I'm going to Spiderwood for the weekend."

"Doubtful."

I snorted. "I'm not asking your permission; I'm stating a fact. Tripp and I have a school project to work on, and we don't want any distractions."

I sighed in relief. Perhaps my life wasn't as fucked up as I thought. I stood up to Mom, yet she hadn't burned me with a cigarette. So, maybe, just maybe, I needed to throw my weight around more. It might've been better if Mom feared me than respected me. Being a bigger bully was sometimes the only way to deal with bullies.

"Why not work on it at his house?" Mom spat, face growing redder.

"Did you hear what I said? We don't want any distractions."

She rolled her eyes. "Like I give a shit about what you want."

"And don't forget Tripp's comment from the other day."

"Excuse me?" Mom asked.

"If you lay one more finger on me, then Tripp will fucking end you," I said.

Mom pushed her sleeves up. "Let him try."

"I'm leaving tomorrow after school and will return Sunday night. But I'll take the guest room at Tripp's house, because it'll probably be late when I return."

"Fine," Mom said through gritted teeth.

"And this is only the beginning," I said. "Things are gonna change around here, and there isn't a fucking thing you can do about it."

Mom shrieked. "Just go."

I approached the coffee table, then grabbed the Beefeater bottle.

A vein surfaced on her head. "What the fuck are you doing?"

I emptied the bottle onto the carpet, then returned it to the table. No harm in this act of cruelty. I just needed to continue driving home how I wasn't some weak little boy, and there'd be serious consequences if Mom continued messing with me.

Mom made a fist. "What the fuck is wrong with you? I don't have any more booze left."

I cackled. "Think of it as the universe telling you to cut back on your drinking."

"You're such an asshole." Mom pointed her index finger at me. "You know what? I'm glad you're going away for the weekend. Means I won't have to deal with you. Although I feel sorry for Tripp. Being stuck with you won't be fun."

"Please. Tripp would never get tired of me," I said. "He's a good person who believes in treating people with respect."

The wind whistled and the trees bobbed the following day at lunch while Tripp and I sat at one of the tables in front of the high school's main entrance.

Tripp's eyes lit up. "You have no idea how happy you've made me by agreeing to our weekend getaway."

The old me might've mocked Tripp for being so forthcoming about his feelings. But I couldn't. Not now. I couldn't get over how someone enjoyed spending time with me. I was human like everyone else, so I couldn't help wanting someone to like me.

Tripp bit into his apple. "Did I say something wrong?"

"No."

"Then what?"

I grinned. "You're a great guy."

The wind picked up more, pushing leaves of red, orange, and yellow into the distance.

Tripp's cheeks flushed. "Thanks."

"There's something I wanted to ask you about Declan."

He finished his apple. "I'm listening."

"There's a rumor going around, and I was wondering if you could clear it up," I said.

"Sure."

"Apparently, Declan might have been dealing drugs."

"That's bullshit," Tripp blurted.

"Really?"

"I'm on the football team, and I would've heard either Declan or one of the guys talking about it."

"Okay. Thanks."

"What made you even ask me that question?" Tripp demanded.

I nibbled on the inside of my lip. "Just wanted you to confirm it wasn't true. I'd hate to think of Declan's name being trashed."

Tripp patted my hand, and I didn't push it away. "Well, don't worry. You'll forget all about the nasty rumor, and everything else once we leave for Spiderwood."

"Absolutely."

Emptiness spread through my body. Lying to Tripp wasn't fun, yet I didn't have a choice. No telling how he'd react if I revealed I suspected

Declan's death wasn't an accident. For all I knew, he'd tell me to drop my inquiry. And I couldn't do that. I didn't have any proof, but this uneasy feeling nagged at me. Like the creepy feeling you get when someone is watching you, but no one is there. The only question was what I'd do next.

CHAPTER 12

Tripp took his eyes off the road for a second and glanced at me. "Still can't believe your mother didn't make a bigger deal out of you leaving town for the weekend."

I adjusted my posture in the front passenger seat. "She's probably getting ready to have a party in my absence."

"Don't say that."

"It's the truth."

"Doesn't make it okay."

"You're right. None of it is okay," I said.

"I'm not trying to rehash anything, but I'm sorry the Sheriff didn't believe you. He deserves to lose his job."

A lump lingered in my throat. "Would it be okay if we didn't discuss my mother this weekend? Isn't that the point of this getaway?"

Tripp remained silent while he barreled down a new stretch of highway. Then, he halted at a red light.

"Sorry," I continued. "I wasn't trying to be rude. I'm just sick of how my home situation seems hopeless."

"I can still help you even if you don't want my family to pay for college."

"What do you mean?" I asked.

Tripp sighed. "Never mind. Forget it."

"If you've got something to say, then say it."

"It's not important."

My throat burned. Perhaps Tripp wanted to ask me something, but was too shy.

Possibly changing his mind about asking me something wasn't terrible, though. I didn't wanna force Tripp to discuss something he wasn't ready to. Perhaps Tripp would mention his comment at a later date. If our relationship blossomed more, Tripp might have the confidence to say whatever was on his mind.

"I've got an idea." Tripp resumed driving once the light changed green. "We should ask each other some getting-to-know-you questions."

"Sure."

"What do you wanna do with the rest of your life if you don't wanna attend college?"

"I always wanted to be a writer."

"That's cool. Have you written anything?"

I bit my lip. "Several things, but I'm sure people would hate it."

I enjoyed writing despite not dwelling on it much. Like writing was my own little secret—something that existed just for my own enjoyment that my mother or anyone else couldn't fuck with. I mean, everyone needed an outlet.

Tripp chuckled. "Don't sell yourself short."

My heart skipped a beat. Tripp once again proved himself even if he wasn't aware of it. His supportiveness was part of why I loved being with Tripp. I would've given anything to have his optimism.

"What about you?" I asked. "Where do you wanna go to college?"

"I'd love to go to Savannah College of Art and Design."

"And where's that?"

Tripp chuckled. "Savannah, Georgia."

"Duh. I'm such an idiot."

"Honest mistake."

"Why would you wanna attend an art school? Gonna give up on sports in college?"

"Yeah. I'd rather focus on my photography."

Wow. Tripp was full of surprises. Although I shouldn't have been shocked. People usually projected the image they wanted people to see. And there must've been a lot I didn't know about him, which was fine. Tripp wasn't my boyfriend—we were just sleeping together. So, he didn't owe me anything. Having some mystery was also nice. I couldn't deny how the conversation interested me. Other than hanging with Gina, Tripp was the only other connection I had to humanity. He was taking the time to get to know me, which was great. Most people would've given up on me a long time ago.

"I didn't know you were interested in photography," I said.

Tripp winked at me. "There's a lot of things you don't know about me."

"Fair enough."

Tripp coughed. "I'd be happy to read one of your stories if you ever wanna share."

"Good to know."

"I'm not kidding, Colt."

My stomach knotted. There Tripp went again, calling me, "Colt." It didn't matter if he did that once or a hundred times. I'd never get over how he had a nickname for me. The gesture was the type of thing that proved Tripp cared about me.

Tripp and I sat at the dining room table at his vacation house several hours later. We decided to get Chinese food—there was a place a couple of blocks away.

I gave him a small smile. "Thanks for suggesting this getaway."

"Not a big deal." Tripp grabbed his spoon, and scooped rice onto his plate. He poured soy sauce on the rice before grabbing a few pieces of General Tso's.

"Sorry. Don't mean to sound pathetic."

He shook his head. "Quit apologizing. You're supposed to be relaxing."

"The same offer goes for you, by the way." I took a bite of General Tso's Chicken. The mixture of the sweet and spicy flavors electrified my taste buds, before I drank some water. "I'd be happy to look at your photographs. If you're comfortable sharing, that is."

"And quit qualifying everything."

"Okay."

"But, yeah. I'd be happy to show you my photography portfolios at some point."

"Fantastic."

Tripp eyed me. "Hope you like your dinner?"

I nodded. "It's great. Best Chinese food I ever had."

"I knew you'd like it. My parents and I can never agree on where to eat, but Lotus Phoenix is the one restaurant we all like."

I raised an eyebrow. "You've gotta be lonely?"

"Pardon me."

"I'm not trying to intrude or anything, but it seems like your parents are strangers in your life," I said.

"You're right." Tripp finished his last piece of chicken, then shoved several more pieces onto his plate. "I'm not that close with my parents."

"You can vent if you want. You didn't judge me."

"I would've listened to anyone," Tripp said.

I gave him a dirty look.

"Kidding," Tripp continued.

"I know, I know."

"My life might seem empty, but I have the football team. Those guys are like my family—I'd do anything for them."

I wouldn't tell Tripp this, but jealousy burned through my body from his comment. I would've given anything to be a part of something and felt like I belonged—like some sort of local writing group. But that'd never happen. It couldn't. It wasn't even because of worrying my mother would ruin it for me. Even if Mom didn't care about me joining a writing group, I doubt they'd accept me. It was a miracle that Tripp accepted me.

"Cool," I whispered.

Tripp leaned closer to me. "Just like I'd do anything for you."

"Glad to hear it."

He laughed, voice echoing through the dining room. "You've gotta pursue your writing dreams."

"And why is that?" I asked.

"Telling your story could help a lot of people. Even if you wanna present your truth as fiction and not a memoir."

I looked away. "Thanks."

"Wasn't trying to embarrass you."

"Don't worry about it. Even I can take an occasional compliment."

Tripp continued his eye contact before wetting his right index finger. He moved closer, then wiped my lip. "You had sauce on your lips," he said.

"Thanks."

I maintained our gaze while my heart thumped louder and faster inside my chest. I couldn't help wondering if Tripp wanted to kiss me.

"Fuck. I'm so glad I met you," he said.

In one swift motion, Tripp kissed me. His hands moved to my cheeks while he pushed his tongue inside my mouth. Maybe, just maybe, my life wasn't so terrible. I didn't have a plan to escape Mom, but I did have these moments of happiness with Tripp. And they were better than anything. If I died tomorrow, then at least I experienced someone's love.

Tripp pulled back from the kiss. "Why don't we clean up and then watch a movie in my bedroom?"

"You've got a TV in your bedroom?" I asked.

"Yup."

My throat tightened despite how Tripp hadn't said anything damning. The differences between Tripp and I would always lurk in the background. Tripp and I were from two different worlds, and I couldn't do anything about that fact. I was poor. He was rich. I didn't know whether I'd live to see tomorrow. Tripp probably didn't even worry about seeing tomorrow because he enjoyed every second of life. And the list went on.

I grimaced. If I wanted to continue my connection with Tripp, then I couldn't keep comparing my life to his. Always juxtaposing our lives might make me resent him. And I couldn't have that. I didn't know what I'd do if Tripp wasn't in my life anymore—that would be a sad fucking day.

Tripp caressed my cheek. "What's wrong?"

"Just want this weekend to last forever."

"I don't blame you."

Tripp and I remained snuggled in his bed. We just finished the movie. So, he grabbed the remote and turned the TV off.

He tilted his head. "Did you like the movie?"

"Yeah, it was nice. Especially with how it had a happy ending."

"Great."

I continued resting my head on Tripp's chest while he stroked my hair. "I've gotta be honest with you about one thing, though."

"Go for it."

"I was jealous of the main character."

"Why?" Tripp asked.

I coughed, clearing the uneasiness from my throat. "The main character had such an easy time coming out."

"That could be you if you wanted," he blurted.

"Come again?"

"I'm not gonna pretend that your situation isn't difficult," Tripp said. "But it won't get better if you don't try."

"Whatever."

"I'd never tell you what to do, but nobody would care if you were gay."

"Actually, I'm bisexual."

"Cool. You can be whatever you wanna be."

"I'm not trying to be difficult—I swear it." I paused. Choosing my next words carefully was a must. I couldn't risk pissing off Tripp. Especially since it was the first night of our getaway. "You've just got no idea what my life is like. Like if Mom is gonna sneak into my room in the middle of the night and murder me in a drunken rampage."

"Sorry, Colt."

"I'm not trying to make you feel bad. I just wish some people would understand how life isn't always easy for some people. Not everyone gets what they want by having stuff fall into their lap or snapping their fingers."

"Ouch."

"I wasn't talking about you," I said.

Tripp heaved a sigh. "I'm proud of you. Confiding in me about your home life couldn't have been easy for you."

I remained silent. Simple statements once again contained profound truths—Tripp was right. Revealing my fucked up home life to him was the most difficult thing I did. Doing so meant giving a piece of myself to someone. Having Tripp know the truth about how Mom treated me meant risking rejection. I wouldn't have blamed Tripp if he didn't want anything to do with me. Running would've been the smart thing to do. Especially since I didn't have anything to contribute to this relationship or offer the world.

"I don't know how, but you'll get through your situation somehow," Tripp continued.

"If you say so."

Chirping birds woke me up the following morning.

I yawned, rubbed my eyes, stretched my arms, then cocked my head. Tripp wasn't in bed next to me.

Deep breaths. Everything had to be fine. Letting my imagination run wild would only harm me. So, I wouldn't do that. I needed to trust my "relationship" with Tripp was fine until there was a reason to think otherwise.

The bedroom door opened, revealing Tripp. He carried a tray, consisting of two plates with pancakes on them, two glasses of orange juice, napkins, silverware, and the maple syrup container. He placed the tray on the bed before hopping on and giving me a quick morning kiss.

"I didn't mean to oversleep," I said.

Tripp frowned. "It's only a little past eight."

"Cool."

"I wanted to make breakfast. Like the first morning in bed we spent together."

I swallowed. I almost kicked myself despite how I couldn't help the thought that popped into my head. I was the luckiest guy in the world. And I was starting to think Tripp told me the truth about his comment last night. About how he would've done anything for me. Breakfast technically wasn't a big deal, but I couldn't help the glee shooting through my body. Tripp couldn't cure me of my abusive home life, but he knew how to make me feel special. And that was something. Most guys might not have been bothered to make breakfast for the person they slept with. I beamed my eyes. "Thank you."

"Hopefully, my pancakes are as good as the first time I made them."

"I'm sure they're great."

"Wait till you eat them," Tripp said.

I sat in a chair in front of Tripp's pool while he was in the water. And except for a couple of stray clouds, the sun shined brightly.

"Don't you wanna join me?" Tripp asked from inside the pool.

"I'm good. You're entertaining me more than you realize by watching you prance around shirtless."

Tripp chuckled. "Nice try."

"Excuse me."

"You're getting wet." Tripp climbed the stairs out of the pool, then walked over to me. He grabbed my arms, forcing me up.

I pouted. "Tripp, please!"

"What's the big deal?"

"Not everyone is as athletic as you are."

"What does sports have to do with it?" Tripp asked.

"Forget it," I said.

His eyebrows inched up. "What? Do you not know how to swim?"

Creepy. Tripp shouldn't have been able to read my mind. Although I shouldn't have been surprised. Spending a lot of time together meant Tripp might have known me more than I realized. And maybe that was okay. I deserved to have someone know the real me.

I remained silent.

"It's not a big deal, Colt. I promise I won't let anything happen to you."

"You can just go back in the pool."

"That's no fun," he said.

My glare intensified. "You might be harmless, but you need to respect my boundaries."

"It's like that night we first met at the party. You said you trusted me before I kissed you, and I didn't misuse that latitude."

Damn. When Tripp was right, he was right.

"I could drown," I said.

"Not on my watch."

I rolled my eyes. "Drop it."

"You'll never get anywhere in life if you keep playing it safe. So, we're doing this." Tripp dragged my arm, and we were in the pool before I could count to ten.

"The water is kind of cold."

Tripp snickered. "Give it a minute."

"You're enjoying every second of this aren't you?" I asked.

Tripp didn't respond, so I craned my neck. Tripp vanished. Something shook the water. Tripp dove up before grabbing me from behind, and wrapping his arms around me.

"Never do that again!" I exclaimed.

"You didn't think something happened to me, did you?"

"Maybe."

"It's adorable when you get nervous." Tripp released me, then kissed the back of my neck. Damn. As if I needed another reminder of how my boyfriend was hot. If I wasn't careful, Tripp might suggest more adventurous things. Like skinny dipping in his pool. Or worse.

"Great."

Tripp sighed. "I want you to know I'd never cross a line—like in the bedroom. I was only having a little fun."

"Don't worry about it."

Tripp flashed a smile. "Hopefully, you're enjoying yourself?"

"I am."

For once, I hadn't put on a façade. My response was true. This weekend was everything I could've hoped for. And I wanted nothing more than to not return to Lakewood the next evening.

"I love you," I blurted out.

Tripp and I were in bed with the comforter wrapped around us. Tripp just rolled onto his back moments earlier and sweat stuck to our panting faces.

His eyes lit up. "I love you, too."

I looked down at the comforter. "You don't have to say it because I did."

"I'm not."

"Really?"

"Yes," Tripp said, nodding. "Don't laugh, but I didn't think it was possible to feel this way about someone."

"Same."

"Thank you for being honest with me."

I let out a breath. "Just because we haven't known each other that long doesn't mean the time we're spending together isn't important."

"Agreed."

I didn't respond. Instead, my eyes remained glued to Tripp. Shock hadn't stopped flooding my body. I needed someone to pinch me. I risked further vulnerability, yet I hadn't been punished or humiliated. And that was a new experience for me. Before Tripp, I never knew honesty could be a good thing.

I turned my head, facing Tripp in the car the following evening. "There's something I'd like to discuss."

"Don't tell me you regret yesterday's love confession." He honked his horn at the car in front of us, then the driver sped down the highway."

"No." I forced a gulp of air into my body. Once I told Tripp what was on my mind, there was no taking it back.

"Promise not to judge."

"I know."

"Although take as long as you want to get comfortable," Tripp said. "We've still got a couple more hours before we're back in Lakewood."

"I'd like you to please help me track down my father," I said.

"Really?" he asked.

"I hope it's okay I'm asking you." I shifted my gaze back to the window. "You just have some resources I don't have. Like what if I need a private investigator?"

Tripp didn't speak.

"What do you say?" I asked.

"Yeah, of course I'll help."

Relief pulsed through my body. Not to be an asshole, but he should wanna help the guy he was sleeping with. It wasn't like I asked for diamonds and a mansion.

"Thanks," I said.

"I've got one question, though."

"Sure. What's up?"

"Why now?"

"Maybe he can help." I bit my nail. "I don't turn 18 till next June. But he's still my biological father."

If I wanted a chance at life, then I'd have to fight for my future. Doing nothing only ensured that my home life would never change. Not like life could get worse.

"Good thinking," he said.

Whether Tripp agreed with me or not didn't matter. This conversation was one of those times when I needed to be told what I wanted to hear. I just needed something, anything to reinforce how I wasn't about to make a gigantic mistake because I knew full well that tracking down my father could leave me disappointed.

CHAPTER 13

Tripp approached me several mornings later while I stood by my locker, getting what I needed for my morning classes. He flashed a brief smile. Then, I zipped up my backpack and closed my locker.

"This a bad time?" Tripp asked.

My stomach knotted. I couldn't help reading into the subtext of Tripp's comment. More specifically, if he was afraid I'd lash out. Being on better terms didn't mean I forgot that morning in the school hallway. I still hated myself for punching Tripp and getting into a scuffle with him—I should've known resorting to violence wasn't appropriate. Yet the rage consumed me in that brief moment. The rage from living with a physically abusive drunk mother. The rage from keeping my sexuality a secret because I didn't want Mom to discover I was bisexual. The rage from why my life couldn't improve.

"No. What's up?" I asked.

"The private investigator got back to me—I have information about your father." Tripp pulled me to the side while several students flocked by.

"Okay."

"He lives in Gingerwood," Tripp revealed.

I blinked several times. Tripp couldn't have made the comment he had. Gingerwood was the town next to Lakewood. And I contemplated the universe's twisted sense of humor. My father could've lived anywhere in the world, yet he was only a fifteen-minute car ride away.

"Is there more?" I asked.

"I have his address. He works at the Gingerwood Diner, and gets home around three. I don't have practice today, so we could do this after school."

"Sure."

He raised an eyebrow. "It's okay if you need more time—I would if I were you. So, I won't be mad if you want to blow this off for a week or two."

Tripp's comment tempted me more than it should've. But no. Talking with my father needed to happen today. More anxiety was the last thing I needed, so I was gonna chat with my father today afterschool.

I bit my lip. "Thanks for doing this."

"You don't have to thank me. I'd do anything for you—I hope you know that."

"I know, I know."

He whistled.

"Something else?" I continued.

"I've gotta say something, but I don't want you thinking I'm being an asshole."

"Go ahead."

"You've gotta prepare yourself for how the meeting might not go well."

My heart pounded louder and faster. The old me might've smacked Tripp for playing devil's advocate but something comforting existed from how Tripp cared about my feelings.

"Are you angry at my comment?" he asked.

"No, it's fine."

Tripp chuckled. "Good. Because making you annoyed is the last thing I wanted to do. We've come too far to backtrack."

"Agreed."

His cheeks flushed. "Now it's my turn to thank you for something."

The way his cheeks turned red was cute. Some people might've wanted to conceal their emotions. But Tripp didn't, proving that corny mantra about some people wearing their heart on their sleeve was true.

"Come again?" I asked.

"Risking your mother's wrath to spend a weekend with me couldn't have been easy for you. So, thanks."

"Don't mention it."

"If you ever need to get away, then we can go back. Just say the word."

I let out a faint laugh. "I'll keep that in mind."

"Good. Because if I'm being honest, then I hope we have another weekend getaway soon. Seeing you so happy was great."

"Thanks."

Joy flooded my body. Something refreshing existed from someone caring about my happiness. For the first time in my life, I was a priority to someone.

Tripp shifted his gaze back to me. "What is it?"

"Thanks for giving me another chance. You're the only person who has ever seen something in me."

"It's called being empathetic. I would've done the same for anyone."

"If you say so."

He gave me a dirty look. "I'm serious, Colt."

"Whatever."

Tripp and I stood in front of my father's apartment building after school while sunlight beamed against the ground.

Tripp bit his lip. "I'll be here for you no matter how this meeting with your father goes."

"Thanks," I mumbled.

Tripp knocked on the door.

"I'm serious." He patted my back, and I didn't shove his hand away despite how we were in public. "Friends" used physical affection all the time, so it didn't have to be the end of the world. It wasn't like he kissed me in front of the whole school.

Footsteps shuffled against the ground, growing louder with each passing second. Showtime.

I stepped in front of my father.

"Can I help you with something?" Clinton asked.

"Do you have a second to talk?" I asked, voice cracking slightly.

"I'm sorry. Do I know you?" Clinton demanded.

I swallowed the lump in my throat. "I'm Colton; your son."

Clinton gripped his tie. "What do you want?"

"Just wanna chat," I said.

Clinton glared at me. "Why?"

"I'm only asking for a couple minutes of your time," I said.

Clinton coughed into his right arm. "Fine. You have two minutes."

"I need your help with something," I said.

The scowl on Clinton's face intensified, yet he didn't say anything. Perhaps I should've been glad he wasn't insulting me.

"My mother is a physically abusive drunk, and I can't take it any longer," I said.

"And that's my problem, how?" Clinton asked.

Tripp eyed Clinton. "Hear Colton out."

"You're my father, and it's not fair you abandoned me," I said.

Clinton snickered. "I did no such thing."

"Huh?" I asked.

"Your mother must not have told you the whole story." Clinton folded his arms. "Your mother is to blame for my absence in your life."

"The fuck are you talking about?" I asked.

"I'm gay," Clinton blurted out.

Mom's homophobia made sense now. Mom would always be a terrible fucking person for how she treated me, yet one fact couldn't be ignored. Her hatred was made, not born. Although despicable, her reason hadn't appeared out of thin air.

"What does that have to do with anything?" I asked.

Clinton grunted. "I told your mother because I couldn't take living a lie any longer. But I offered to stay married to her for your sake. She refused and threw me out of the house. I even tried sending child support checks for the first year or two, but she returned them."

I shook my head. Mom might've been a terrible fucking person, but I couldn't see her turning down free money. "You're lying," I said.

"I'm not—I can show you the checks," Clinton said.

"So, what?" I snapped, voice growing louder. "You gave up on me?"

"It's not like that," Clinton said.

I put my hands on my hips. "Then what was it like?"

"I had to save myself," Clinton said.

"And you didn't care if I was collateral damage?" I asked.

"Sorry," Clinton whispered.

I screamed. "Do you have any idea what it's like to be burned with cigarettes or constantly beaten? I go to bed every night wondering if I'll still be alive in the morning."

"Don't know what you want me to say," Clinton said.

"I want you to be sorry for not fighting for me," I said. "Imagine if you had custody of me instead of my mother."

"Not like I can fight for custody now. No court would give me custody after not being in your life for over a decade." Clinton ran his fingers through his brown hair while the sunlight shined against it, almost making it look dark blond.

I made a fist, tears welling in my eyes. Time to purge my feelings. It wasn't like life could get worse.

"I don't deserve to be abused," I said.

Clinton pressed his hands together. "I'm sorry. But there's nothing I can do."

Clinton started walking towards the apartment building's door.

"Not even if I told you I was bisexual?" I called out.

Clinton tilted his head. "I'm so sorry. Best of luck to you."

He entered the building after another word and was soon out of sight.

I sobbed while tears dripped down my face. I couldn't believe it. Tripp was right. My brilliant plan to chat with my father backfired, and I'd have to do what I always did. Live with the pain.

Tripp opened his arms, inviting me in for a hug. I collapsed against his body, burying my head in my chest while he rubbed my back.

Having my father insult me wouldn't have been as bad as him being indifferent about my existence. But no. It was as if I was a stranger to him. And if I was gonna escape Mom, then I needed to find another option.

Tripp scooted closer to me in bed hours later. Then, he looped his arms around me, cuddling me. Sweat clung to our faces while we caught our breath.

"Thanks for inviting me over," I said. "Just didn't feel like being alone after what happened earlier."

"No problem."

"Thank goodness my mother believed me when I texted her about spending the night at a classmate's house so I can work on a project."

Tripp scrunched his eyebrows. "You think she believed you?"

"Probably too drunk to care."

Tripp nibbled on the inside of his lip. "There's something I've gotta tell you."

"Okay."

"I wasn't honest with you."

"About what?" I asked.

"I lied when I said Declan wasn't dealing drugs—he was."

Wow. Perhaps life wasn't a complete disaster. Whether I accepted the fact or not, the universe handed me a gift. I might not have dwelled on Declan that much recently, but his death still lingered in the back of my mind. Like with how he was too clumsy to accidentally shoot himself. The only problem was my amateur sleuthing had gone cold. Hard to continue investigating when I didn't have any leads.

I wiped a bead of sweat from my forehead. "Why be honest now?"

"I don't want there to be any secrets between us," he said. "Whether our relationship is in private, or public doesn't matter—we need to be able to trust one and another. Do you hate me?"

"I could never hate you, Tripp."

"Really?" he asked.

I averted my gaze. "You forgave me for punching you even though most people wouldn't."

"Not a big deal."

"Most people would worry about us turning into an abusive relationship," I said.

"While I get what you're saying, our relationship isn't a group project."

My eyebrows knitted together. "Meaning?"

"We're the only ones who matter in this relationship—nobody else's opinion matters"

"Fair enough."

"There's one thing I've gotta know, though." Tripp caressed my hair. Something intoxicating existed from Tripp showing me physical affection. "Why did you care about some rumor about Declan dealing drugs?"

I stared at Tripp for the longest minute of life. Tripp was right about trust needing to exist between us. So, it was time to tell him my theory about Declan's death. And it didn't matter if he mocked my theory regarding Declan's death being a murder, not an accident.

"I don't think Declan's death was an accident," I said. "He doesn't seem like the type of person who'd shoot himself from being tipsy."

Tripp's jaw twitched. "What are you saying?"

"I think he was murdered."

CHAPTER 14

I sat at a table in the back of VERONICA'S the following day after school. Gina was across from me, yet I remained silent despite how it'd been a good minute since she returned with our lattes. Gina might've been my childhood best friend, but I couldn't ignore her scowling. More specifically, how she could've been upset about it once again taking me so long to return her text messages.

"I'm glad we're finally gonna catch up." Gina grabbed her steaming mug but placed it back on the table. "And we could've hung out sooner if you hadn't been avoiding me."

I averted my gaze. "Not avoiding you."

"Yeah, you are, and it's okay. You aren't Mr. Social. So, I've gotta accept that if we're gonna make this friendship work. Either that or you're trying to punish me for how we drifted apart once I started attending private school."

"I know." I sipped my latte, then looked up at her. "What's new with you? How's the college application process."

She grinned. "A lot better than the last time we talked. I've got my choice of schools narrowed down."

"That's amazing."

Gina leaned closer. "What about you? Given more thought to the future?"

I shrugged. "College isn't for me. Not like I'd get in anywhere."

She glared at me. "You got a 2300 out of 2400 on the SAT."

I slid my elbows onto the table. "Doesn't matter. My grades are shit."

"You just need to start caring more." Gina held my hands. "You deserve more than to die in this small town."

"That's a morbid thought."

"It's the truth. You can't seriously be content with being an assistant to your mother?"

I pulled my hands away from her. "Don't mention my mother."

"Sorry. My bad."

"I do have one piece of good news."

Her eyebrows shot up. "Cool. I'd love to hear it."

"Tripp and I are still going strong."

Fuck. I was more of a softie than I realized. Gushing about the guy I was "dating" was the type of thing a normal person did. For a moment, at least, the euphoria from gawking about Tripp felt good. Because I wanted more fun in my life. Like holding hands, having breakfast with friends, or laughing.

She twirled a strand of hair around her finger. "Thought you said he wasn't your boyfriend, and that you two were only a sexual thing?"

My shoulders tensed. "Boundaries blur."

She giggled. "I'm glad you haven't fucked things up with Tripp."

"Gina!" I exclaimed.

"Not trying to be harsh. But anyone with half a brain can tell you're like a cactus."

"No need to state the obvious."

"Tripp treating you right?" Gina asked.

"Shouldn't you be asking the opposite?" I asked.

"Hope things continue going well with him." Gina drank more of her latte, then she nibbled on her chocolate chip cookie.

"Thanks," I mumbled.

She pointed her finger at my cheeks. "Look at you! Your face is red!"

Gina would be the death of me. She just lived for embarrassing me. And that was the last thing I needed. It wasn't like I teased her much.

"No need to make a big deal about it," I said.

"Have you met me?" she asked.

"Whatever."

Gina's chest expanded and contracted while she inhaled and exhaled several deep breaths. "There's one more thing I wanted to say."

"And what's that?" I asked.

"I can help you with coming out if you're worried about people not accepting you. But I'm sure most people won't care. And even if people gave you flack, they'd move onto something new soon enough."

"Gina, please!"

Her gaze shifted to her cookie. "My bad. You're still not ready for this, and that's okay. Just know I'll be here for you when you wanna take the next step."

Thank goodness Gina took a hint. We might not have hung out all the time, but I didn't know what I would've done if Gina pushed the subject about me coming out. There was a good chance I'd do something stupid—like lashing out. And I couldn't have that. Gina was the only one other than Tripp who saw there was a real person beneath my rough exterior.

I returned home from hanging out with Gina an hour or so later, discovering Mom sitting on the living room couch. A bottle of her gin and glass were on the table in front of her.

I snorted. "Bad day?"

Mom stood. "You better shup the fuck up, boy!"

"You don't scare me."

"Excuse me?"

"I'm not afraid of you."

Her eyes bulged, accentuating their menacing green color. "And where the fuck you've been? Out being a faggot with that Taylor loser?"

"His name is Tripp."

She gripped my shoulders, digging her nails into me. "Admit you're a faggot!"

I shoved Mom off me before she stumbled backward, almost falling. Then, I screamed. I was gonna do this. I was gonna tell Mom that I was bisexual. Because I didn't care if the idea sounded trite or cliché. Experiencing joy and love from Tripp made me wanna be a different person. Someone who was no longer complacent in their own abuse. Mom needed to know I wasn't some scared, little boy. Since I was almost eighteen, I was practically an adult. A man.

I yelled louder. "So what if I like guys? The fuck are you gonna do about it? If you've got a problem with me being bisexual, then that says more about you than me."

Her lips curled. "I knew you were a faggot. I just knew it."

"You're nothing but a sad, pathetic, bitch." I cackled. "And I know more than you think."

"The fuck you talking about, boy?"

"You hate me because Dad was gay," I said.

A brief euphoria once again flooded my body. I couldn't help myself. Mom needed to know the days of pushing me around were over. I was seventeen, not five. With one simple comment, I exposed the root of Mom's hate and abuse. And there wasn't a fucking thing she could do about me calling her out on her bigotry.

"How the fuck do you know that?" Mom demanded.

"Doesn't matter."

"You're a disappointment. Hope you know that."

Mom punched me, then I fell. One punch wasn't enough, though. Mom pinned me to the ground and kept hitting me. Over. And over. And over again before I finally shoved her off me.

I threw her against the ground before kicking her several times.

"I can fight back too!" I exclaimed. "You're a fucking pathetic excuse of a person, and I hope you drop dead of a heart attack. It'd be the best thing that ever happened to me."

Mom coughed. "If you feel that way, then you better not sleep here tonight."

"Gladly!"

I sat on a stool in Tripp's kitchen half an hour later.

The microwave beeped. Tripp removed the plate filled with macaroni and cheese from the microwave, then handed it to me.

I smiled. Just couldn't help finding comfort in the simple moments. Like how the person I was sleeping with cared more about providing me with a decent meal than my mother.

I sipped my water before taking a bite of food. "Thanks for picking me up."

"Don't mention it."

"I'm serious."

He chuckled. "The least I can do. Especially since my parents aren't home. I hope you like the mac and cheese."

"It's great!" I said.

"You can tell me if you hate it."

I almost laughed. "You're more neurotic than I realized."

Tripp didn't respond. Instead, he chugged his Gatorade.

"Only a joke," I continued.

"I know, I know." Tripp returned his focus to me. "Although I've been thinking a lot about the Declan Thing."

"If you've got a suggestion, then I'm happy to hear it."

"We need to go to Declan's house after school one day. I can chat up his mother, and you'll excuse yourself to go to the bathroom."

Whether Tripp realized the truth or not, he was hotter than I imagined. I didn't want Tripp to be a thug, but his scheming and thinking about Declan's death revealed he had a mischievous side. He didn't mind bending the rules every now and then. And that was great, because we needed to do whatever it took to solve Declan's death. It was the only way we'd get closure.

"But I'll be searching his room?" I asked.

"Yup," Tripp said.

"You think searching his room is the key to unraveling everything?" I ate the last bite of macaroni and cheese, then grabbed a napkin. I wiped my lip before shoving the napkin and plate to the side.

"If Declan was murdered, then it could be because of dealing drugs," Tripp said. "Like a disgruntled client haggling over a price or a rival dealer."

Thank goodness Tripp hadn't mocked or teased me about thinking Declan's death wasn't an accident. I meant what I said about not being afraid to listen to ideas. I was only one person and couldn't play amateur detective by myself. Not when my shitty little investigation hadn't gotten anywhere.

"Anyway, I was wondering if you'd wanna watch a movie?" Tripp asked.

I nodded. "Sure. That'd be great."

CHAPTER 15

I stood in Declan's bedroom the following day after school.

Tripp had morning practice today as opposed to afternoon practice, so he accompanied me and distracted Declan's mother. The only problem was I hadn't discovered anything that could be useful. His room was the same as usual. His bed was unmade, papers and notebooks cluttered his desk, dust covered his bookcase, and most of his clothes were in his hamper. It appeared as if Declan's parents couldn't deal with going through his stuff and deciding which things they wanted to save and which they wanted to donate or discard. And I didn't blame Declan's parents for their possible trepidation. I would've hesitated if I were them. Declan's room was the last thing they had left to hold on to him. I almost left Declan's bedroom when a folded piece of paper on top of a notebook on Declan's desk caught my attention. I grabbed the note, then unfolded the paper and read it:

Meet me in the woods behind your house at 10PM the night of your annual New School Year Party or there's gonna be trouble. You might have everyone else fooled, but I'm not drinking the Kool-Aid. Someone is dead because of you, and that's not okay. Better to chat with me than   ruin your precious image. Trust me, Declan. I'm not someone you wanna mess with.

Kisses,

BF

Someone knocked on the door. My pulse soared, then I cocked my head. Tripp stood in front of me, not Judy. So, I was fine.

I furrowed my eyebrows. "Please don't sneak up on me again."

"Sorry. Didn't mean to startle you."

"Everything okay?" I asked.

"Judy had to pick up her husband from the airport, so she told me that we can just let ourselves out when we finish our tea and cookies."

"Cool."

He folded his arms. "Find anything useful?"

"Yeah. I did."

Tripp chuckled. "Don't leave me in suspense. Distracting Declan's mother by rambling about my fear of cats better be worth it."

"He met with someone before he died," I blurted.

"Come again."

"I'm serious, Tripp." I handed him the note.

He handed it back a moment later. "Interesting. Perhaps there's more to your theory than I realized. So, kudos to you."

I wrinkled my nose. "What? You doubted me?"

"I didn't want you to get your hopes up."

"Fair enough," I said.

"What are you gonna do with the note?"

It was the first real lead I got in Declan's death. The initials were a good start, but there could've been dozens of people who lived in Lakewood with the initials BF.

"I'm gonna keep it," I said.

"Think that's the best?"

"It's evidence that Declan could've been murdered. What if Declan's parents throw out the note by mistake?"

He sighed. "You've got a point."

"Thanks. I love it when we're in agreement."

Tripp stuffed his hands into the pockets of his varsity jacket. "Careful about using the L-word. I might think we're in a real relationship."

My stomach sank—I couldn't help feeling slightly guilty by Tripp's comment. I wasn't oblivious to how he probably wished we could take our relationship public in addition to how my actions impacted other people, mainly Tripp.

He gave me a look. "No snarky comment?"

"Nope."

"I'm shocked."

"Anyway, I'm ready to go whenever you are," I said.

"Sure. No problem."

My teeth chattered. I rubbed my hands together, creating friction.

"Something wrong?" Tripp asked.

"Just colder out than I realized."

"You're only wearing a tee-shirt."

I almost curled my fingers into a brief fist. Violence wasn't the answer, yet I couldn't help being annoyed by Tripp's comment. Abusive parents—like Mom—could also be neglectful. So, I was lucky that I even had the clothes I did.

"So?" I asked.

"Maybe you should think about dressing for the season." Tripp chuckled louder. "We're already well into fall and it'll be winter before you know it."

I snorted. "Whatever."

"Here." Tripp removed his varsity jacket, then placed it on me.

"You don't have to give me your jacket."

"What? Not good enough for you? Or are you embarrassed to be wearing something of mine?"

"It's not that."

"Then what?" he asked.

"I don't want you to catch a cold."

Tripp pointed at his shirt. He sported a long-sleeve Henley tee-shirt.

"Unlike you, I dress appropriately for the weather," he said.

"Very funny. But we should go before Declan's parents return and catch us snooping in his bedroom."

I returned home from school a couple of days later, finding Mom in the living room drinking. "Come here, boy!" Mom exclaimed. "We need to chat."

I obeyed Mom no matter how many hairs on my back stuck up from the sound of her voice. Still best to let Mom say whatever she wanted to say. Especially when it didn't take much to make her overact.

"Yes?" I asked.

Mom stood.

"I wanna apologize," Mom said, slurring her words.

I must've been living in an alternate universe. Mom would've rather died than apologized to me. That was like saying the sun and the moon were the same thing. It just didn't make any sense, and I was gonna have to be careful about how I navigated this conversation. Mom could be "nice" one second and batshit crazy the next.

"For what?" I asked.

"I should've been a better mother to you. I know it's not your fault that your piece of shit father abandoned us."

"Okay?"

She looped her arms around me, gin breath pricking my skin. "And I promise things are gonna be different. Just because I hate faggots doesn't mean I've gotta resent you. Who knows. Maybe you can have Tripp over for dinner one night."

"We're not dating."

She cackled. "Doesn't matter what you call it. My earlier comment stands. Anyone can see he's crazy about you."

I hated how Mom saw through me. There was a small amount of truth to what she said. I didn't have to label Tripp my "boyfriend" in order to care about Tripp, because I didn't know what I would've done without him.

"What game are you playing?" I asked.

"I'm not fucking around—not this time."

"I don't believe you."

"You're the only family I have, so I might as well try and tolerate you." Mom paused for a beat. "Even if the thought of you sharing a bed with another guy creeps me out more than the liquor store running out of gin."

"Thanks," I mumbled.

"You don't expect me to believe you went out of town that weekend just to work on a project, do you?"

My shoulders tensed. Mom might have been a lot of things, but I had to be careful. She clearly had some brain cells left despite all her years of alcohol abuse.

Tripp's parents were still out of town the following evening, so that meant going over to Tripp's house after school. And currently, I was in his bed while he cuddled me from behind.

"There's something I've gotta tell you," I said.

"Shit. And here I thought we were having a nice moment," Tripp said.

"I promise I'm not mad," I said.

He chuckled. "Good."

"My mother knows I'm bisexual," I blurted.

"What the hell?"

"I'm not kidding. The truth just kind of came out in addition to how she gave me a drunken apology the other day."

"That's cool."

"What? Nothing to say?"

Tripp continued spooning me. "If she was drunk, then I wouldn't believe her apology. Not like your mother is gonna change into a good person. At best, she's feeling guilty for how she treated you. No offense, or anything."

"You're right."

"But, hey. You always have me."

"I know, I know."

"Promise me you'll be careful with your mother?"

"Promise."

"Good. I don't know what I'd do if anything happened to you," he said.

My breathing finally slowed down. Interesting how Tripp and I felt the same way despite how we weren't dating.

"Thank you for not being angry with me," I said.

He chuckled, voice tickling my right ear. "What are you talking about?"

"I'm not trying to start trouble by giving you an out, but I know this dynamic isn't fair to you. You must wanna take me on a real date like to the movies or out to dinner."

"Doesn't matter how we're spending our time together. The point is, we're spending time together, and that's enough for me."

Tripp held me tighter while rain pattered against the window and wind slammed into the house. Tripp and I might not have had forever, but we had this moment. And that was something. Not fighting about taking our relationship public proved Tripp gave me something I needed—unconditional acceptance.

CHAPTER 16

I halted before the turn in the hallway the following morning at school—I just got the textbooks and notebooks I needed for my morning classes. Two people were arguing at the end of the hallway, and I stole a glance at them. And they were too engaged in their disagreement to realize I peaked at them. One of the people was Declan's best friend—Warren Jameson—and the other was Blair Flynn. Blair was a senior like Declan, Tripp, and me.

"Do you understand how much trouble I could cause?" Blair asked.

Warren pouted. "Please don't do anything rash. Declan's memory doesn't deserve to be desecrated. Who gives a fuck if he was a drug dealer? He's dead now."

"Doesn't matter," Blair said.

"Are you doing this to honor Thomas or are you doing this for yourself?" Warren demanded.

Blair flipped her hair over shoulders. "Doesn't matter that it's been six months since Thomas died. Declan sold him the drugs that he overdosed on."

I pulled back from the turn in the hallway, so I was now hidden from their sight. I didn't have to be perfect to realize that Warren and Blair might eventually notice my presence. And I couldn't have that. I didn't need to be an actual detective to understand the importance of discretion.

Blair hissed. "Thomas would be alive if it weren't for Declan."

"That's not fair and you know it. If it wasn't Declan, then it would've been someone else who dealt him Marci."

Marci. That was the latest designer drug going around Lakewood. I only heard whispers of it, but I'd never consume the drug. The side effects of Marci were said to rival that of Molly. And I only hoped there'd be no more overdoses.

"Doesn't matter," Blair said.

"I can give you money if you want."

She snorted. "My father is the CEO of a biotech company."

"Never hurts to have enough money," Warren said.

"Really think Declan would do the same if roles were reversed?" Blair asked.

He grunted. "We were brothers."

"That's laughable, and you know it. He'd throw you under the bus in a heartbeat."

"That's not fair, Blair."

"Just being honest. Not my fault you can't accept it."

Warren exhaled a breath. "Hating Declan is one thing, but do you really wanna subject Declan's parents to additional misery?"

"It's what they deserve."

"They didn't wish for Declan to die."

I scratched my chin. Something clicked in my mind. The initials of the person who sent Declan the note were BF, and those were the same initials as Blair. And if her boyfriend died of a drug overdose, then that would've been motive enough for her to meet with Declan the night he died. Maybe they had a heated argument, and she shot him and made it look like an accident.

"Whatever," Blair quipped.

Warren snickered. "Have you forgotten what I know?"

"Not sure what you're getting at."

"I know you met with Declan in the woods before he died," Warren said. "Maybe you shot him in a fit of rage."

I was gonna have to be a little more thankful. Blair meeting Declan in the woods the night he died was no longer a theory. The only question was if Blair was capable of killing someone. Even an accident would've required being pushed to an extreme emotional state. She couldn't have insisted Declan meet her, only to shoot him. If she was this upset over Thomas's death, then she probably wanted to at least have a conversation. Chatting with Declan would have been her last grasp at closure. And a small part of me understood that feeling. Latching onto fleeting moments and opportunities was sometimes the only thing a person could do.

"It's not a crime that I happened to be around Declan when he was using the cans to practice shooting in the woods," Blair said.

"You better fucking shut your mouth—you don't have any proof," Warren said. "Don't need evidence to try you in the court of public opinion."

Blair shrieked, creating an echo. "Fine! I won't do anything for now."

"Good."

Footsteps grew louder, then someone glared at me. It was Warren.

"Were you spying on our conversation?" he asked.

I bit my lip, drawing blood. A metallic taste filled my mouth. So much for not wanting Warren or Blair to catch me. If I didn't think of an explanation, then my life could get more complicated. And I couldn't have that. Not if I wanted to continue investigating the truth about Declan's death.

"No. Just had a panic attack," I said.

He shook his head. "Whatever. I don't have time to waste on a freak like yourself."

Tripp and I laid in bed the following evening, facing each other.

Taking a shower and freshening up wasn't Tripp's only problem. His lips remained curled. So, I only hoped that I didn't do anything to piss him off.

I elevated my eyebrows. "Everything okay?"

"There's something I wanted to ask you."

"We've slept with each other numerous times, so there's no need for you to be bashful. If you wanna ask me something, then you should."

"Sure."

I chuckled. "Out with it."

"I'm not trying to pressure you, but I was wondering if we could go out on a date. We don't even have to call it a date—we could think of it as an outing. We don't even have to kiss or hold hands."

I remained silent.

"Like see a movie or something," Tripp continued.

"I see."

"I won't be pissed off if a public outing makes you uncomfortable. I don't wanna force you to do anything you aren't ready for."

Tripp was a keeper. Most teenagers might only focus on their own feelings, but Tripp seemed prepared to sacrifice his own happiness to please me.

He looked down at the bedroom comforter. "I didn't offend you, did I?"

I elbowed him. "Don't be ridiculous."

"What do you say?"

I took in several deep breaths. On the one hand, I couldn't forget Mom could relapse back to her violent and homophobic ways despite her "apology" the other day. On the other hand, I'd never be happy as long as I continued being secretive and caring about what others thought. Mom also knew I was bisexual and seemed to realize Tripp and I were an item.

I nodded my head. "I'd love to go to the movies with you."

Tripp gave me a quick kiss on the lips. "That's fucking awesome. And you have no idea how happy you've made me."

The old me might've teased Tripp for sounding corny or caring too much. But not now. I'd come too far. I wasn't certain of much, but I had zero doubt about one thing. Life changed on a moment's notice, sometimes for the worse. Like with Declan. One minute he was alive. And the next minute he was dead. Life could also change for the better, though. Like with Tripp's presence in my life. Sometimes meeting the right person was all it took to have a different outlook on life.

"Good. I'm glad," I said.

Tripp gave me a mock frown. "And don't even think about offering to pay. I asked you out on the date, which means I'm paying for the tickets, popcorn, soda, and food if we go out to eat later."

I could've rolled my eyes or whispered some expletive. But I didn't; I couldn't. I'd be damned if I let my pride get in the way over something silly as who'd pay for the date. Besides, I needed Tripp to pay for our outing. I didn't exactly have pocket money.

I approached Blair the following morning by her locker at school.

Her locker clanked shut. She then gave me a dirty look when I coughed, clearing my throat. I wouldn't blame her, though. The old me would've been pissed off if a stranger accosted me.

"Can I help you with something?" she asked.

"I need to ask you a question, and I need you to be honest with me."

She ran her fingers through her blonde hair. "Don't even know you—nobody. That's the problem with being a loser."

"I know you met with Declan in the woods the night he died."

"So?" Blair asked.

"Did you kill him? Maybe the conversation spiraled out of control, and you made an impulsive decision."

She cackled. "Like when you attacked Tripp that day in the hallway?"

"I'll leave you alone if you answer my question," I said.

"Fine." She pushed her backpack strap further up her shoulder while several students darted down the hallway. "You win."

"Well?" I demanded.

"Nope, I didn't kill him. But I wish I did."

"And why should I believe you?"

"I got pulled over by a Lakewood cop when I left the party, which was right after my chat with Declan. And I can give you his phone number if you wanna verify."

"Drunk driving?" I asked.

"For speeding, asshole!"

I raised my palms at her. "Sorry."

Blair grabbed a hair tie from her pocket, ran her hands through her hair, then placed it in a ponytail.

"Anyway, we're done." Blair walked away from me without another word.

I dug my fingernails into my backpack straps. Blair might've been rude and borderline belligerent, yet my gut told me she wasn't lying. An officer being on duty was something that could easily fall apart if she lied.

More students and teachers trekked down the hallway, then the warning bell echoed. But I didn't move. If Blair didn't kill Declan, then I needed a new suspect. It didn't matter if my theory was only a hunch. Declan's death being ruled an accident still seemed too convenient. And I'd have to act quickly.

Tripp and I went to the movies several afternoons after my conversation with Blair. And fortunately for us, an elderly couple were the only other people in the theatre.

He leaned into my ear. "I hope you're enjoying the movie."

"I am," I whispered.

"Good."

I almost grabbed a handful of popcorn when my hand brushed up against Tripp's. "My bad," he said. "You go first."

"No worries." I scooped the popcorn with my hand, then munched on it. The buttery flavor electrified my taste buds, then I drank more soda. Nothing like a snack to make me thirsty.

One of the main character's friends in the movie got stabbed to death sometime later, and I yelped. Being stabbed was a terrible way to go because of how a person might linger for a beat while bleeding to death whereas a gunshot wound could be instantly fatal if the person knew where to shoot.

I placed my head on Tripp's shoulder without thinking, and he didn't push me away. Instead, he held me.

"Sorry," he mumbled. "Should've warned you it was gonna be a scary movie."

The old me might've argued with Tripp about him choosing such a scary movie. But I didn't. Not when the enjoyment from a first date flooded my body. For this moment, only Tripp and I mattered.

I held his hand, and I allowed myself to forget about all my traumas. Like my mom, and Declan being dead. Or how I didn't see Gina as much as I should've. Sitting alone in the theater with my head on his shoulder, I finally accepted that I enjoyed how Tripp made me happy.

CHAPTER 17

Tripp and I sat by his bedroom desk doing homework after school. Today was one of the days Tripp had morning practice, so I jumped at the opportunity to hang with him. Even if we were doing schoolwork instead of having sex.

I scribbled something in my notebook, then cocked my head at Tripp. "Thanks again for our date in December."

"You don't have to thank me for spending time with you."

"Not because of that."

His eyebrows swung up. "Then what?"

"Going to the movies and out for pizza two months ago was exactly what I needed."

"The date must've been good if you're still thinking about it." He continued typing on his laptop. "Has your mother started backsliding?"

"Not yet. But I'm sure she will soon enough."

"I should be thanking you too."

"And why is that?" I flipped to the next page in my math textbook. "You're the one who spoiled me."

"Holding my hand in the theatre couldn't have been easy."

"We don't have to make a big deal about it."

"I'm not. I just appreciate the effort," Tripp said.

"Most people wouldn't be patient with me. They'd probably cuss me out and wish me dead."

Tripp winked. "I'm not most people. So, stop living in your head and enjoy the moment. It's what I'm doing."

"Point taken."

"These last few months have been the best months of my life." He looked up from his laptop, then kissed my lips.

"Mine too. I didn't know happiness was possible."

"You just needed the right people in your life."

"I only have to make it to graduation," I said.

Tripp returned his attention to his laptop's screen. "You aren't gonna be an assistant to your mother at her real estate business?"

I didn't even hesitate. "Nope."

Yup. I meant what I said. I deserved happiness, and I wasn't gonna let Mom fuck with my life anymore. She couldn't stop me from leaving home once I was eighteen.

"When did you decide this?" Tripp asked.

"A couple of weeks ago."

"And you're only telling me now?"

I shrugged. "Just nervous to mention it."

"Relax. I'm teasing."

"I know. I know."

Tripp clenched his jaw. "How'd you reach this decision?"

I shrugged. "I just realized I needed to do what is best for me."

Tripp sighed. "I'm really sorry about your investigation."

"It's not your fault—I'm the idiot. I'm too lazy to take the initiative."

"Not lazy to take a pause."

"I just don't know what to do," I said.

"Is it possible Declan's death was an accident?" Tripp asked.

"Maybe," I mumbled.

"I'm sure Declan would be flattered that you care so much about his death."

"Don't know about that." I shoved my textbook and notebook to the side. "Can you think of anyone else who would have a motive for killing Declan?"

He whipped his head back and forth. "Nope."

"Fair enough." I rested my hand under my chin. "Just can't believe Christmas passed. And then New Year's. And then Valentine's Day."

"You and me both."

The door opened. A woman in a gray pantsuit entered Tripp's bedroom. Tripp glared at his mother. "What the hell?" he asked.

"You're supposed to keep your bedroom door open when you have company," she said.

He chuckled. "I'm eighteen, which means I can do whatever the hell I want."

She giggled. "Watch your language!"

"Whatever," Tripp said.

Tripp's mother put her hands on her hips. "At least tell me you were polite enough to ask your guest if he wants to stay for dinner."

Tripp bit his lip. "Mom!"

Tripp's mother walked over to me, then shook my hand. "I'm Izzie."

"Colton," I said.

Izzie blew a loose strand of hair to the side. "We're having prime rib and mashed potatoes for dinner."

"Colton actually has to leave soon," Tripp said.

"No, it's okay. I don't have anywhere else to be," I said.

Tripp glanced at me. "Sure?"

"Yeah. It's not every day that I get to have prime rib," I said.

Tripp rolled his eyes. "Very funny."

Izzie rubbed her hands together. "Fantastic. I can't tell you how pleased I am that you're having a friend over for dinner."

"Mom!" Tripp exclaimed.

"I'm actually not his friend—I'm Tripp's boyfriend," I said.

My heartbeat hadn't increased from what I said. I had no regrets about calling Tripp my boyfriend. Taking small steps with accepting myself was better than doing nothing. It wasn't like Tripp's mother would post about our relationship on social media or gossip about us to her girlfriends. Tripp's mother seemed nice enough, because my standard was pretty low. If I didn't get beaten up or burned with a cigarette, then I'd consider the day to be a win.

Izzie gripped her pearl necklace. "That's cool. Anyway, I'll holler when dinner is ready. Should be no more than fifteen or twenty minutes."

"Sounds good," I said.

Tripp's mother exited the bedroom, then left the door open behind her. Tripp waited before her footsteps were no longer audible before coughing.

"You don't have to stay for dinner," Tripp said. "We don't have to be like normal couples and have you meet my parents."

"Not a big deal."

Tripp looped his arms around my shoulders before meeting my gaze. "I'm proud of you for not being afraid to admit you're my boyfriend."

My heart almost skipped a beat. I sometimes couldn't help myself. Like with how it was nice Tripp believed in me.

"It's fine," I said.

Tripp clenched his jaw. "It's okay to take a minute and talk about your feelings. I wouldn't blame you if your head was filled with a bunch of contradictory emotions."

"I'm good."

"I really couldn't be happier." He pulled me in for a bear hug. "Accepting yourself is the best present you could ever give me."

Happiness washed over me. Sometimes, I surprised myself. I hadn't anticipated having dinner with Tripp and his parents. But maybe a shakeup was what I needed. It was sweet that Tripp wanted to protect my privacy. However, I'd never truly be living my life if I always played it safe.

Tripp and I sat next to each other at the dining room table, while Izzie sat next to him, and Tripp's father—Roger—sat next to Izzie.

Stereotypes could sometimes be offensive, but Tripp's family proved rich people cared about appearances. Like with how two lit candles stood in the middle of the table in addition to how they used a velvet tablecloth.

Izzie sipped her red wine before looking in my direction. "Hopefully, you like dinner? Prime rib is one of my favorite meals."

"I can't believe you're actually home," Tripp said. "You and dad must be gone at least twenty to twenty-five days out of the month."

My throat constricted. Sympathizing with Tripp couldn't be helped even though his parents hadn't done or said anything bad. Tripp might've always plastered a smile around school, but I couldn't deny how he was human too. Like with how he understood what it was like to be lonely. Everything had a price. And with Tripp, that meant not seeing his parents much must've been the price he had to pay for such a fancy lifestyle.

"When you're right, you're right." Roger ate a spoonful of mashed potatoes. "Tell me something, Colton." Izzie grabbed a napkin, then wiped a bit of mashed potatoes from her lip. "Do you have prime rib a lot?"

"He's more of a pizza and sandwiches type of guy," Tripp said.

Running interference was smart of Tripp. His parents might've been better than Mom, but I couldn't ignore the obvious difference. They were rich and I was poor. And if I wasn't careful, conflict might arise.

"That's cool." Izzie finished the remaining wine in her glass, then poured a refill. "I had the best sandwich when I went to Italy several years ago. Only problem is I can't remember what was in the sandwich."

I laughed. "That is a problem."

Izzie continued looking at me. "What do you like to do, Colton?"

"I'm a writer." I ate the last bite of my prime rib, and the salty aroma lingered on my tongue. And that was great. Nothing wrong with being a foodie. Great food deserved to be savored.

"That's fantastic," Izzie said. "One of my best friends is a writer. Perhaps she could give you a referral to her literary agent if you're interested."

"Yeah. I'd like that," I said.

My pulse lowered slightly while we became engrossed in further conversation. I couldn't deny how overwhelming this whole happiness thing was. This moment—dinner with Tripp's parents—was what I wanted more out of life. So, maybe I was slowly becoming a believer. Perhaps happiness was possible, after all.

I handed Gina her latte the following afternoon at VERONICA'S.

I sat down across from her, then dunked my lips on the whipped cream and caramel drizzle before taking a big sip.

She patted my hand. "How's everything going with you and Tripp? Please tell me you haven't fucked things up?"

"Everything is fine." I drank my latte. "We might not be public yet, but I took a small step yesterday."

The placard clanked against the door, then a lady with white hair entered the coffee shop. I was more concerned about the wind that just swooshed inside of VERONICA'S, though. An icy sensation washed over my body, proving how March was coming in like a lion.

"How so?" Gina asked.

"I met his parents."

Her pupils dilated. "Seriously?"

"It was a moment of serendipity." I coughed, clearing the uneasiness from my throat. "But I'm more interested in chatting about you. Sorry I forgot to congratulate you about being accepted to Columbia."

"No worries. Liking my Facebook status was enough."

"Parents must be thrilled?" I asked.

Her shoulders slouched. "Not really. Columbia is just what was expected of me. Anyway, back to you."

Fuck. I should've known Gina would find some way to make me the focus of the conversation again. Mild embarrassment was what she did best. And she only got away with it because she was my best friend.

"Why am I always in the spotlight?" I asked.

"Because I worry about you." She leaned closer. "So, hopefully the intensity around Declan's death has lessened."

"It has."

She gripped her ponytail. "Good."

CHAPTER 18

I approached Tripp's locker before first period. I tapped his shoulder, then he whirled around. He greeted me with a smile before closing his locker.

"Hi," Tripp said.

"Would it be alright if I kissed you?"

"Feeling okay? I wouldn't expect you to wanna be so open in public."

"It's what I want. If you're comfortable with a PDA, that is."

"What about if word gets back to your mother?" Tripp asked. "Telling her your bisexual and people knowing her son is bisexual are two different things."

"Fuck it. I don't care."

He blinked. "Seriously?"

The chattering of voices echoed through the hallway, and that only meant one thing. It must've been only a couple of more minutes before the warning bell would ring for first period.

My Adam's apple bobbed up and down. "I'm tired of being a coward. You deserve a real relationship."

His smirk widened. "I want you to go public with our relationship because you want to. Not because you feel obligated to."

"Understood."

"Then, yeah. I'd love a kiss."

I pulled Tripp in for a kiss without considering the matter any further. No point in prolonging the inevitable. Stalling could also make me change my mind. And I couldn't have that. Not if I wanted my life to be about living and not just surviving. Clichés once again contained profound truths. I could only be young once, and I didn't know what I would do if I looked back five years from now, overwhelmed with regret.

We pulled back from the kiss after another beat. Various voices filled the air. Everyone remained huddled in their various cliques, and nobody even glanced at us. So, my sexuality might not have been as big of a deal as I thought it was.

"So proud of you," Tripp said.

"Thanks."

Glee radiated through my body because I just couldn't help my reaction. Making someone—other than myself—happy was a good thing. It meant Tripp saw something in me. And I'd revel in the feeling. Important to enjoy the nice moments while I could, because it didn't matter if Mom limited her toxicity to snide comments and hadn't hit me or burned me with a cigarette in a long time. Declan's death still proved how life was fleeting. If Mom didn't kill me, then something else might. So, I'd enjoy my time with Tripp while I could.

The bell rang.

"Walk to first period together?" Tripp asked.

"Only if I can hold your hand."

"Go for it."

I grabbed Tripp's hand, then we headed down the hallway.

For once, my pulse wasn't vibrating in my ears, and I couldn't be more thankful if I tried. Life wasn't as scary as I thought. Almost as if there was hope for recovery. Because I had to be honest with myself. I never felt as free as I currently was while holding hands with Tripp. In this moment, I was living life for myself. And that was all that mattered.

"If I had known dinner with my parents would make you more comfortable, then I would've suggested it a long time ago," Tripp said.

"Yeah. Last week changed things."

We turned the corner in the hallway, then made a left before strutting down a new hallway.

"There's something else I wanted to ask you," I continued.

"You wanna get engaged?"

"Not exactly."

"Then what?" he asked.

"I was wondering if you'd be willing to take me out on another date?" I tilted my head, then shot him a brief apologetic look. "I'm sorry that that movie and pizza date was the only public date we've had."

He squeezed my hand tighter. "Please don't apologize for being yourself. I wouldn't be with you if I didn't like you. I might be nice, but I'm not that nice."

Tripp had a point. I should've had more faith in our relationship. Tripp and I might not have had a conventional relationship, yet we were still together after all these months. And that   counted for something. Words and labels were nice, but I didn't need them to tell me what I wanted—Tripp.

"You didn't answer my question," I said.

He turned his head, now facing me. "Sure. I'd love to take you on a date. You know I'd do anything for you."

"Same."

"But remember progress isn't always linear. It's okay if you feel uncomfortable or have doubts several days from now." Tripp drew in a breath. "And I wouldn't judge you for that. Not ever."

Damn. Tripp must've really known me well since he was being so patient and understanding with me. However, I wanted this. To kiss him in public. To hold hands with him on the way to class. To have dates. To stay up all night talking about life after one of our trysts. To attend prom together. To even continue spending time together once high school ended. I died a little death every day in the past thanks to Mom. But not now. More and more of me was being brought back to life thanks to Tripp.

Tripp and I had our date the following day after school.

I settled on wanting Tripp to take me to VERONICA'S. It was the perfect spot for hanging out because it was low-key. Not much pressure existed from having a latte and splitting a big cookie.

"Hopefully, this was a good idea?" I asked.

He rubbed my hand. "Don't care where I am. Just care that I'm with you."

"Thanks."

"I'm serious." He broke off part of the chocolate chip cookie, then munched on it. "Pressuring you is the last thing I want."

"And I'm thankful for that."

He chewed on the inside of his lip. "There's something that worries me."

"What'd I do?"

"I just worry about your grades."

"I have a C+ in all of my classes." I planted my lips on the whipped cream and caramel drizzle. "And that's fucking fantastic compared to the beginning of the school year."

"True. Forget I said anything."

Footsteps wobbled against the ground. Something coughed, and I looked up. My stomach almost became tangled in my throat. Running into Clinton was the last thing I expected to happen while out on a date with Tripp.

I shot him a menacing look. "Can I help you with something?"

"I had to say something." Clinton rocked his hands back and forth. "I know it's been months since we talked, but I feel terrible about our conversation."

I stood, then continued glaring at him. "And what? Do you expect me to absolve you of your guilt? That's never gonna happen."

"I don't expect you to like me," Clinton said.

I made a fist before unclenching it a moment later. I wasn't that guy anymore. The me at the beginning of the school year might've decked Clinton. I couldn't, and not even because Tripp would be disappointed. The anger wasn't worth it. Those types of emotions were only reserved for Mom.

"You haven't told me what you want?" I asked.

"Just wanna apologize," Clinton asked. "I can't imagine what a nightmare your mother has made your life. And for that, I'm sorry. You're just an innocent kid and deserve the same thing as any other teenager."

"Are you done?" I asked.

"Yeah. And again, I'm sorry for everything you've gone through." Clinton sipped his coffee before walking out of VERONICA'S without another word. I sat back in my chair once Clinton was finally out of sight.

Tripp pushed the plate with the cookie on it towards me. "You can finish the cookie. You deserve it."

I shoved the plate back at Tripp. "It's fine. We can share it."

"You must be having a lot of thoughts."

Yeah, my stomach lurched. My father surprised me big time moments earlier—I got an apology without even asking for one. "Yeah," I mumbled.

"You can vent if you want."

"I'm good. But there's something else I wanted to run by you."

"Go ahead." Tripp finished the rest of his latte. "Promise not to judge."

"The Declan situation is still nagging at me."

"Understandable. He was your first friend at Lakewood High School."

I furrowed my brow. "You don't think I'm pathetic?"

"I'd never think that." Tripp drummed his fingers against the wooden table. "Anyway, what's your idea?"

"We need to go back to the scene of the crime."

"Come again?"

"Maybe we'll find something that was overlooked." I expelled the longest sigh of my life. "But if we don't, then I promise to drop the matter."

"How am I involved in this?" he asked.

I finished my latte. "I'd like you to come with me. And I know you must be worried about being arrested for trespassing. If Declan's mom or dad catches us, then we can say you're looking for a lost possession in the woods."

"From last summer?" Tripp asked.

"Got a better plan?"

"No, yours actually sounds smart."

Thank goodness sweat didn't drip down my face. I didn't know what I would've done if Tripp criticized me for wanting to check the woods behind Declan's house. Being my boyfriend meant Tripp was the one person who was supposed to believe in me. Even when I sounded dumb. Even when I had no idea what I was doing. Even when I didn't deserve latitude. Because I would've done the same for him.

***

The wind whipped through the air while sunlight poked through the cloudy sky several afternoons later.

Tripp and I were in the woods behind Declan's house. However, the cool temperature wasn't the reason for how my stomach might as well have been in my throat. The frown lines on Tripp's face indicated he might've been ready to give me a lecture. Like it was time for me to accept how Declan's death was an accident.

I wouldn't accept defeat, though. Not when a red cap sticking out of a pile of leaves a few feet away from me stole my attention. I walked over to the pile of leaves and kicked them to the side.

No amount of time could've prepared me for what I found under the pile of leaves. Only one discovery would've given me goosebumps. A single serving shot size bottle of Beefeater gin. As in the type of gin Mom drank. As in the type of thing she might've drank while on the go. As in the type of thing that might've been my first real clue about Declan's death.

Tripp placed his hand on my back. "What's wrong, Colt?"

I flashed the shot size bottle of Beefeater gin at Tripp. "I think my mother killed Declan."

CHAPTER 19

I sat at a table in front of my high school finishing homework a couple of days after discovering the mini bottle of Beefeater gin in the woods behind Declan's house. Tripp gave me a quick kiss on the lips, then sat next to me.

"Hi," I said.

"We need to chat." Tripp munched on an apple. "And I'm not gonna let you change the subject, because this is important."

I looked up at Tripp for a second. "Did I do something wrong?"

"I didn't wanna push the topic at first, but we don't have a choice." He ate more of his apple. "Have you confronted your mother about the bottle of booze?"

Tripp should've known better than to ask that question. I was a lot of things, yet I wouldn't start trouble with Mom unless absolutely necessary—life had been calm at home lately. No telling what would happen if I accused her of killing Declan.

"No," I stammered.

"Good. Because you need to forget about the discovery."

"You think I'm crazy, don't you?" I asked.

"Don't be ridiculous."

"That's what you're implying," I said.

"You've made so much progress with your life, and it would be terrible if that was ruined because of one chat with your mother."

"Have you forgotten what I said?" I asked.

Tripp sipped his water. "You're gonna have to be more specific."

"Her car was in a different spot when I returned home the next day after our tryst."

"You don't have any concrete evidence," Tripp said.

"I know, I know."

He placed his hand over mine. "Promise to drop this? I'm only being so insistent because I care about you. I mean, I'd love us to be able to take our findings to the police, but we'll end up looking like the crazy ones without concrete proof. A bottle of booze only places your mother at the scene of Declan's death."

"There's something you don't know," I blurted.

"Don't tell me you killed Declan and are framing your mother?" Tripp asked.

I gave him a dirty look. "Don't be silly."

"Then what?" Tripp asked.

"Declan knew I was being abused and wanted to do something about it."

I tilted my head while the trees bobbed in the wind. A squirrel darted across the grass before climbing up the tree. Being an expert at keeping secrets wasn't only about hiding my sexuality from Mom and the rest of the world for all these years. Declan was privy to my toxic home life, and I now had to deal with whether or not I was indirectly responsible for his death, because the scorching sensation in my stomach was starting to eat at me.

Declan and I stood in his bedroom a week before his party—the one he died at. Except Declan and I weren't gonna just play video games or binge on junk food and soda like we usually did. Not if he didn't stop looking at me.

"What?" I spat.

"You aren't fooling anyone."

My gaze narrowed. "Don't know what you're talking about."

"The black eye is fresh because you didn't have that the other day when we hung out." Declan pushed up his sleeves.

"If you have something to say, then don't hold back."

"Is your mother abusing you?"

I looked away. "Why would you ask that?"

"Your father isn't in the picture..."

"So, what if my mother is abusing me?" I remained silent, unable to swallow the lump in my throat. I couldn't believe I was doing this. I was gonna confide in someone about my turbulent home life. "Not like anyone can help me."

He whipped his head back and forth several times. "You're wrong. A tragic ending isn't inevitable for you. I'm gonna hire you an attorney to help you get emancipated. And if you feel uncomfortable with me paying for it, then I'm gonna help you find one who accepts pro bono cases."

"Why do you care?" I asked.

"You're my friend and deserve a decent future."

"Did you actually get an attorney?" Tripp interrupted while he shifted his posture.

"No."

"It isn't your fault Declan is dead."

My attention returned to my notebook and textbook. "There's more."

"I'm afraid to ask..."

"I gloated to my mother the next day about Declan helping me become emancipated."

The wind roared louder and faster, nipping our faces. I was full of surprises, and at some point, I'd have to examine whether keeping all these secrets was healthy.

Tripp scrunched his eyebrows. "Please don't blame yourself, Colt. You aren't responsible for your mother's actions—that's on her."

"Thanks," I whispered.

He gave me a funny look. "I'm serious."

"I know. I know."

"I'm proud of you for wanting justice for Declan, but you've gotta keep living your life too."

My stomach coiled. Tripp's words lingered in my mind despite how he hadn't meant anything bad. He was right, but I couldn't shake the niggling inside me. Declan was dead and I was alive. And my guilt intensified. Just because I didn't think about Declan all the time didn't mean I didn't care about our friendship. Finding out the truth about his death was to honor his memory. Yet somehow, without even realizing it, I'd become so consumed by my relationship to Tripp that it felt like Declan was never alive.

I returned home from school the following day after my blunt chat with Declan, only to find Mom by her usual spot. Sitting on the couch with a bottle of gin and glass on the living room table.

"Where the fuck have you been, boy?" Mom bellowed.

I shuffled into the kitchen. "I was in school. Maybe you'd realize it was a weekday if you weren't such a lazy drunk."

Mom took a drag from her cigarette, then stubbed it on the ashtray in front of her. After that, she stood. She charged towards me, grabbed my shoulders, then shoved me against the living room wall.

"You better start showing me some respect otherwise I'll burn you with a cigarette," she said. "And you wouldn't want that, would you? I remember all your screaming last time and would hate for history to repeat itself."

"This ends today, you fucking bitch." I yanked Mom off me, then smacked her against the carpet. I even kicked her twice. Once would've been enough, but I added an extra kick for good luck.

"You're gonna pay for that, boy!"

I leaned closer, then almost spat in her face. "Make me!"

Mom remained silent.

I snickered. "Wait. Don't tell me you're too intoxicated to stand up? If you are, then you might wanna cut back on the drinking. You aren't doing your liver any favors."

"Screw you!"

"Declan Price is helping me find an attorney so I can get emancipated, and there isn't a fucking thing you can do about it." In one swift motion, I stepped on her right hand. Something cracked. Hopefully, it was her bones.

I removed my foot from her hand. Then, I tilted my head. Her glass—the one she used for her gin was scattered, shards in various spots. Damn. I hadn't stepped on her hand as hard as I thought I had.

She made a fist with her left hand. "I told you not to hang out with that loser!"

I kneeled in front of Mom. "Newsflash. I stopped listening to you a long time ago."

"You're gonna pay for this one day. Perhaps burning you with cigarettes was kind. Yeah, next time I'll water-board you in the toilet. How does almost drowning in a toilet sound?"

"Go to Hell!"

Tripp patted my back. "Please don't let your mind wander. Gloating to your mother doesn't mean she killed Declan."

I stretched my hands out on the table. "You don't think it's possible she snuck out to the party, searched the woods for Declan, confronted him, stole his gun, then shot him?"

"I don't know."

"It's not like I want my mother to be guilty of killing Declan—she already has enough to pay for."

He continued rubbing my back. "I'll support you whatever you decide to do, but please consider the consequences of your actions?"

"Yeah. I know she might go ballistic and kill me if I accuse her of killing Declan."

Tripp forced in a breath. "It'd kill me if anything happened to you, Colt."

"Good to know you care." I pushed his hand off my back.

"What are you thinking?" Tripp asked.

"I'm sorry, but I can't promise I won't confront my mother," I said. "Declan deserves justice."

"He wouldn't want you to wreck your life for him."

"We don't know what he would've wanted," I said.

"Come again?"

"I'm sorry to say this, but Declan wasn't the person I thought he was," I said.

Tripp made a clicking noise with his tongue. "Are you referring to how he dealt drugs? Everyone does stupid shit when their young."

"Getting drunk at a party is stupid shit. Dealing drugs is just plain reckless."

Tripp scoffed. "He defended you when nobody else would."

"I know," I mumbled.

"You sometimes have to take the good with the bad."

Whether I liked Tripp's comment or not, he was right. Most people weren't all good or all bad. They were somewhere in the middle. It was possible for good people to do bad things and for bad people to have moments of good. The only thing that mattered was what was in Declan's heart. But I wasn't psychic, so I'd have no way of knowing that.

My shoulders tensed. Lunch time wasn't the time for life altering philosophical conundrums—they'd only make my head throb.

Tripp stared me down. "Life might be scary right now, but I promise everything will be fine. Just have a little faith."

"Don't make promises you can't keep."

"I'm not."

"How can you be certain everything will be okay?" I asked.

Tripp remained silent for a good minute or two while his chest expanded and contracted faster. "Because the alternative is worse."

I sat at a table after school in the back of VERONICA'S. Except it wasn't just Gina and I hanging out. She brought her boyfriend, Neal with her.

"I'm glad we're doing this." Gina nibbled on her croissant. "You have no idea how hard it is to get a hold of this one."

I gave Gina a dirty look. "I show up eventually."

"I'm teasing," Gina said.

Neal sipped his hot chocolate, then tucked a loose curl behind his ear. "It really is nice to meet you, Colton."

"Same." I drank more of my caramel latte. "Although you haven't told me the most important part of your relationship."

Gina bit her lip. "And what's that? You better not ask some awkward question."

"How did you guys meet?" I asked.

"On the Columbia admitted students Facebook group. I mean, I kinda always had a small crush on Gina. But I was too shy to approach her." Neal took his glasses off after grabbing a cloth from his pocket.

Then, he wiped his glasses. "I still can't believe they accepted two students from the same school."

"Neal is a classmate?" I asked Gina.

"Must've forgotten to mention that." Gina chugged the rest of her latte. "You know how forgetful I am."

Neal squeezed Gina's hand. "No big deal."

I took a bite of my sugar cookie, letting the crumbs linger on my tongue before swallowing them. The mixture of the sweet, buttery, and doughy flavors lit up my taste buds. There was just nothing like a good sugar cookie.

"Do you know what you want to major in, Neal?" I asked.

"No," Neal said.

I flashed a smile. "No big deal. You'll figure it out."

Thank goodness Neal didn't know what he wanted to study in college. The curly hair and glasses kind of made him a nerd. And knowing what he wanted to major in would've been the last straw. If I wanted to be a dick, then I would've teased Gina about dating someone below her social strata. That was the thing about opposites, though. They sometimes complemented each other.

"What about you?" Neal asked.

"Sorry?" I asked.

Neal finished his hot chocolate. "Do you know what college you're going to or what you wanna major in?"

"I'm not attending college," I said.

Neal blinked. "Seriously?"

"Yup," I murmured.

Gina glanced at her boyfriend. "Colton has always been a free spirit."

"I respect that. I'd give anything not to care about society's expectations," Neal said. "Shit I can't imagine how liberating that must be."

"Yeah. Certainly unconventional," I said.

Neal rambled while joy filled my insides. More moments like these were what I wanted. Some people might've hated mundanity, but I didn't. Meeting my best friend's boyfriend was the type of thing normal people did. Because in this fleeting moment, I wasn't the kid with a fucked up home life. I was just having a carefree afternoon.

CHAPTER 20

I returned home from school, and my heart thumped louder and faster. Mom wasn't in her usual spot on the living room couch. So, I couldn't help my rising back hairs. Drinking during the day might not have been smart. But there was a certain comfort in routine. Even with someone as depraved and demented as Mom. Finding her on the couch each day was about needing to know her whereabouts at all times.

I walked into the kitchen because I was thirsty. And I almost screamed. Mom stood in the kitchen, smoking a cigarette.

"What are you doing home?" she asked.

"School is over for the day."

She gasped. "Oh."

"We need to talk."

"You better not say anything disrespectful—I'm not afraid to burn you with this." She waved the cigarette at me, then took a drag. A plume of thick smoke left her mouth, and my heartbeat increased more.

Tripp wouldn't like what I was gonna do, yet I didn't have a choice. I needed to know if Mom killed Declan. Even if Mom might go ballistic from the accusation. It wasn't like she could do anything to me that she hadn't done before. So, I'd be fine. I hoped, at least.

"Did you kill Declan Price?" I asked.

She gave me a dirty look. "What the fuck kind of question is that? Have you been taking stupid pills again?"

I folded my arms. "Your car was parked in a different spot when I returned from Declan's party the following day."

"So?" Mom took one last drag on her cigarette, then stubbed it in the ashtray on the kitchen counter.

"But that's not all."

"What the fuck you talking about?"

"I found a mini bottle of Beefeater gin in the woods behind Declan's house."

Her face turned pale. Damn. Hating Mom and not wanting to be right about her killing Declan were two different things. I could intellectualize how Mom was a terrible fucking person. But that didn't mean I thought she was capable of murder. If she murdered Declan, then there was nothing good about her. Declan was only a teenager, after all. There was just something really evil about killing a kid.

"Well?" I demanded.

She grabbed another cigarette from her pocket, then lit it. "Yeah, I killed that fucking son of a bitch. You're welcome."

I believed her. If she were playing mind games, she'd do it in a way that made me suffer as much as possible. Watching me squirm from her confession was far more gratifying.

"Why?" I asked.

"Do you even have to ask?" Mom exhaled smoke before taking an even longer drag. "He was gonna help you become emancipated, and I couldn't have that."

"He was only seventeen."

"Doesn't matter. I wasn't gonna let you leave me."

"Let me guess. You wiped your prints and placed the gun in his hand to make it look like an accident?"

Mom nodded. "And I'd do it again."

"How did you get a hold of the gun? Was there a struggle?"

"It was on a tree stump in front of him. He must've put it down so he could finish the rest of his drink."

I scrunched my eyebrows. "How did you even know where Declan would be?"

"I heard some people at the party mention he was in the woods. Something about how he likes to practice shooting cans to clear his head."

"You don't feel bad Declan is dead?"

"He got what was coming to him."

Mom cackled, and goosebumps clung to my body. I shot her a confused look. I didn't understand what was funny. It wasn't like someone told a morbid joke.

"Something you wanna share?" I asked.

"You know why I'm confessing this, right?"

"No. Why?"

"You have no proof I killed Declan." She put her cigarette out on the ashtray. "A bottle of booze won't send me to jail."

I hated when she was right. For all the police knew, the bottle of Beefeater belonged to anyone and might've been from an earlier party. And even if they did DNA testing and found her saliva under the cap, that still wouldn't send Mom to jail. Because Tripp was right about his earlier point. It was a big leap between a bottle of booze and having concrete proof Mom killed Declan.

I grunted. "Declan was my only friend, and you took him from me."

"You're doing fine."

"The fuck does that mean?"

"You have Tripp in your life, so you've got nothing to complain about."

"I hate you!" I exclaimed.

She wrinkled her nose. "I'd have to value your opinion to get upset at what you just said, but I don't."

"Whatever," I mumbled.

"I bet you're kicking yourself for not recording this conversation?"

I made a fist. Mom was once again right. I should've planned this conversation better. If I were smart, then I'd get a recording and try blackmailing her with the confession. But no. Somehow, I allowed hubris to win.

"And I'm not gonna confess again," Mom said.

"Never say never. Maybe I catch you when you're drunk, and you end up spilling your feelings."

"I have a better chance of becoming the pope."

"Declan did more for me than you ever did. Hope you know that."

"You can insult me as much as you want, but it won't matter."

I lunged closer to Mom. "I'd be careful if I were you. I might not have a recording of your confession. But I don't need one."

"Maybe it's time to check into a sanitarium."

I snickered. "You're gonna have to be more specific."

"You have no leverage. As far as the world is concerned, it's as if this conversation never happened."

"The court of public opinion is different from winning a trial."

"Good luck," she said.

"Declan's parents must be in Hell."

"That's their problem."

"Why are you so cruel?" I asked.

I couldn't help the question. And it didn't matter if I grasped at something that wasn't there. Mom couldn't have been born evil. So, I wondered if something fucked up happened to her. Something worse than Clinton being gay.

"That's a stupid question."

"It's not"

She twisted a strand of hair around her finger yet remained silent. Perhaps she answered my question without technically answering it. Some people were cruel because they could be.

"You better at least answer my next question," I said.

"Knock yourself out."

"Did you seek Declan out with the intention of killing him?"

She didn't blink. "Yeah, I wasn't gonna leave the woods until Declan died. And I would've felt bad about wanting him dead. But he kept going on about how he was gonna get you emancipated and that there wasn't a fucking thing I could do about it. What a prick. Please. As if I'd let some rich, preppy teen boss me around."

"He was a human being."

Mom shrugged. "Oh well."

Tripp and I laid in his bed the following evening.

My conversation with Mom meant going against Tripp's wishes, but I escaped unscathed. And I only imagined how angry Tripp would be when I told him what I did. "There's something I've gotta tell you," I said.

His lips quivered. "Don't tell me your mother hit you again?"

"Not exactly."

"Then what?"

"I confronted my mother about whether she killed Declan, and she confessed everything." I looked away from Tripp. "You're probably gonna be pissed with me, but I don't care. I needed to do what I did."

He sighed. "How could you be so stupid?"

"Excuse me?"

"What if she burned you with a cigarette or hit you?" Tripp asked.

"She didn't."

"That's not the point, and you know it," Tripp said, speaking louder. "You know your mother isn't someone to fuck with."

A lump lingered in my throat. "I needed to know the truth finally. You understand that, right?"

"At least tell me you recorded her confession so you could use that as evidence?" Tripp asked.

"No," I mumbled.

"What the hell is the matter with you, Colt?" He paused for a moment, exhaling louder. "Imagine if you could force her to turn herself into the police."

"Mom said the same thing."

Tripp remained silent.

"So, what? Do you hate me now, and are you gonna breakup with me?" I asked.

He raised a brow. "Are you for real?"

"I'll understand if you hate me and want nothing to do with me. I'd feel the same way if I were you."

Tripp scooted closer, then placed his hands on my shoulders. "I'm not gonna end things because I disapprove of something you did."

"Really?'

"It's possible to disagree with someone, but still love them."

Love. I'd never get used to Tripp saying that. Hard to believe someone cared about me. There wasn't much to like about me. Especially when I could be stubborn and do whatever the fuck I wanted such as my conversation with Mom proved.

"You're too important to me to lose." Tripp hugged me, then I closed my eyes. Tears dotted my eyes. Tripp didn't just love me. He'd tolerate almost anything, because that was part of what unconditional love was.

"You too," I said.

We detached from the hug, then he bit his lip.

"Don't tell me you're crying?" Tripp asked.

"Allergies fucking suck."

"Don't worry, Colt. I won't tell anyone you have a sensitive side."

"You better not."

Tripp cracked his knuckles. "Did you at least get the closure you wanted?"

Damn. Tripp knew how to ask a loaded question, because I wasn't sure how to respond. On the one hand, I was privy to the truth about Declan's death. On the other hand, chatting with Mom confirmed my worst fears about her. Mom was the way she was, and that was all there was to it.

I couldn't forget how knowing how Declan really died wasn't the same as getting justice for Declan and his family, though. Knowledge wasn't always power. Knowing Mom killed Declan was just something I'd have to live with.

"You don't have to answer my question," Tripp continued.

"Cool."

"But I'm curious about what you're gonna do with the truth?"

"Live with it like I do everything else," I finally said.

CHAPTER 21

I exited VERONICA's after school when a black SUV approached the curb. The front passenger seat window rolled down, then I snorted. It was Clinton.

"Do you have a sec?" Clinton asked.

"I've got nothing to say to you."

"You're gonna wanna listen to what I have to say." He sighed. "It'll only take five minutes of your time. Promise."

Clinton had some nerve asking to chat—even if he wanted to help me. Just couldn't forget how I wouldn't have suffered abuse all these years if he hadn't disappeared from my life. What Mom did to me was an abomination, and she deserved to burn in Hell.

"Will you leave me alone after this?"

He nodded.

"Fine." I walked over to the SUV, opened the door, then slammed it behind me. "What's up?"

He bit his lip. "I've got a present for you, and you better accept it."

My shoulders tensed. Clinton wasn't the boss of me. So, I didn't have to do a fucking thing he said. He never acted like a real father. Nope. He lost that opportunity. "Sorry. Wrong choice of words," Clinton continued.

I shifted my posture in the front passenger seat before something stole my attention from the corner of my eye. A brief case was on the car floor in front of me. Interesting. Perhaps this was Clinton's gift.

"I was bought out of the Gingerwood Diner," he revealed.

"I didn't realize you were one of the Gingerwood Diner owners."

"There's a lot you don't know about me."

My glare intensified.

He coughed into his right arm. "I got four million dollars from being bought out. And there's three million dollars in that briefcase."

I still had no idea what he was about. "Why did you wanna sell your stake in the Gingerwood Diner?" I asked.

"Looking for a change."

"How can someone afford a four-million-dollar buyout for a diner?"

"My business partner is wealthy, but that doesn't matter," Clinton said. "The only thing that's important is that the money is yours."

Clinton couldn't have said what he had. The universe wasn't this generous. So, he must've pranked me. Clinton was playing a game. Other than Tripp and Gina, people weren't kind.

I blinked. "Really?"

"And you can do whatever you want with the money."

"Why not keep the money for yourself?" I asked.

"You deserve a fresh start after everything you've gone through."

I narrowed my gaze. "What's the catch?"

"There isn't one," Clinton said. "Although I hope you'd be smart enough not to tell your mother about the money."

"I'm leaving home once I graduate. I'm not gonna die in some small town."

"Hope the money helps."

"I don't have to ever talk to you again?" I asked.

"Nope." A couple of tears rolled down Clinton's face. "But for what it's worth, I'm sorry I didn't fight for custody of you. Giving up and abandoning you was wrong, but I know nothing can undo the past."

"Thanks."

"What about that guy?" Clinton asked.

"Come again?"

"The one you were with when we chatted both times?"

I grunted. "We're not doing this. Don't get me wrong. The money is great. But I'm not gonna share intimate details of my life. I'm sorry, but you aren't entitled to those facts."

"Understood." He put his hands on his lap. "But please take the money. Everyone needs occasional help."

I didn't have to think twice about accepting Clinton's offer. There was being stubborn. And there was being stupid. Nothing good would come from rejecting Clinton's money. If Tripp and I were gonna make our relationship work beyond high school, then I needed to somehow support myself. I wouldn't be able to live with myself if I leeched off Tripp for the rest of my life.

I snatched the briefcase from the car floor. "You don't have to ask me twice. I'll absolutely take the money."

"Good."

"I should go." I opened the car door, then Clinton grabbed my arm.

"Wait!" Clinton exclaimed.

I titled my head back to Clinton. "What?"

"The combination on the briefcase is 714," he said. "Anyway, good luck. Hope you get everything you want out of life."

"Thanks," I mumbled before almost stumbling out of the car.

I closed the door behind me before Clinton drove away.

My heart almost leapt out of my chest. I shouldn't have had a lump in my throat from the idea of never seeing Clinton again. But I was only human. And for one fleeting moment, I wondered what life would've been like if Clinton acted like a real father.

Tripp couldn't stop shaking his head at me while we were in bed, catching our breath. Hopefully, I hadn't pissed him off in some way. I didn't know what I would've done if I wrecked the one good thing in my life.

"Something wrong?" I asked.

"Kind of pissed at you."

"The fuck you talking about?"

"You took Clinton's money, but you won't take mine?"

I picked my nail. "This has nothing to do with hurting you. In fact, this isn't even about you. Just doing what I needed to do."

Tripp bit his lip. "I've offered to help numerous times. But maybe you're too stubborn to realize that."

"The last person who helped me was murdered," I said.

"I'm not afraid of your mother."

"Whatever."

"You do realize your mother is probably gonna lose control of her temper at some point soon, right?"

"I can handle insults."

"Not what I'm talking about," Tripp said.

My stomach coiled. "No offense, but it's ridiculous how you're making everything about you. I needed help dealing with my mother, and I got it. That's all that matters. And if you loved me, then you'd be glad I found a solution to my problem. The only thing I ask is that you let me keep the briefcase here."

"Seriously?"

"Don't trust my mother."

"But there's a combination," Tripp said, "I also don't need a reminder of how you let your absentee father save the day but you'd rather die than let me assist you."

I snorted. "Wow. Someone has a big ego."

"Doesn't matter if I have a high opinion of myself. Loving you and doing whatever it takes to make you happy isn't a bad thing."

"I don't wanna fight."

"We've had this conversation before, Colt." Tripp cracked his knuckles. "Couples sometimes fight."

"This isn't just about escaping my mother," I blurted.

Tripp's eyebrows swung up. "I don't understand."

"Accepting my father's money means I can contribute something to this relationship."

"You know I don't care about that stuff. This isn't a competition." He heaved out a sigh. "But if it makes you feel better, then I won't discuss the money again."

"Cool," I said.

Relief washed over me. This disagreement with Tripp was another moment of opening my eyes. We bickered, yet the world hadn't ended. And that was the exact opposite of the life I grew up with.

My stomach grumbled.

"Why don't I order a pepperoni pizza for dinner?" Tripp asked. "It'll be my treat."

"Sounds good."

"Great. Glad you aren't fighting me on this."

I chuckled. "I'll never turn down free pizza."

Sweat dripped down my back while Neal, Gina, Tripp, and I sat at a table in the back of VERONICA'S.

Didn't matter how many times someone pinched me or threw cold water in my face. I couldn't believe I was on a double date—like a normal teenager. And it felt great. If I wanted my progress to continue, then I needed more moments like these. Moments when I believed escaping Mom was possible. Moments when I believed the universe wasn't as cruel as I suspected it was. Moments when I believed nothing else mattered in the world besides my happiness.

Gina giggled. "Thank goodness we didn't have to twist Colt's arm to do this."

I sipped my latte, then glared at Gina. "Only Tripp is allowed to use my nickname."

Tripp elbowed me. "Lighten up."

"Whatever," I said.

Neal nibbled on his cookie before glancing at Tripp. "It's cool you're interested in both sports and photography. I might be stating the obvious, but I didn't realize that was possible."

Tripp stretched his arms out on the wooden table. "Yeah. Life isn't always black and white, and it's important to realize that."

Neal grinned. "Philosophical too; I like it."

"It's great Colt allowed himself to be vulnerable with you, Tripp," Gina said. "He can't stop talking about you whenever we're together."

"Gina!" I exclaimed.

Tripp eyed me. "Always great knowing you care."

"Don't be silly. I've never lied about my feelings for you," I said.

"We should have another double date sometime soon," Gina said.

"That's fine by me," I said.

Gina's eyebrows shot up. "Really?"

"Yup." I sipped my latte, then finished eating my cookie.

"I can't believe high school is almost over," Neal said.

"You're too young to be nostalgic for high school. You haven't even graduated yet," Gina said.

Neal's cheeks turned bright red. "Can't help it."

I laughed before I could stop myself. Neal would make for an interesting character in a story. Nostalgia seemed to be a common problem in life, and understandably so. Change was sometimes scary. But it was also necessary. Such as with me moving away from home after graduation, for example. I needed to put as much distance between my mother and me as possible.

CHAPTER 22

Tripp and I sat by his desk, doing homework after school. He jotted something in his notebook, then shoved his notebook and textbook to the side. After that, he coughed.

"Everything okay?" I asked

"There's something I've gotta ask you, but I don't want you to think I'm pressuring you for a commitment."

I smirked. "I won't bite. So, say whatever is on your mind."

"I got into Williams University."

I furrowed an eyebrow. "I thought you wanted to attend Savannah College of Art and Design?"

He snickered. "Good to know you pay attention. But yeah. I did wanna go there. Although I didn't get in."

"Don't be ridiculous. I always pay attention."

"I'm not sure about that..."

"What'd you wanna ask me?"

"Williams University is my next choice after SCAD," Tripp said.

"Okay."

"It's in Los Angeles."

"That's cool. Definitely would definitely be interesting living on the west coast."

Tripp exhaled. "Maybe I need to be more direct."

"What are you talking about?" I asked.

"I'm asking you to move to LA with me. I plan on getting an apartment close to campus, so we'd have privacy."

I didn't even have to contemplate Tripp's offer. His proposition was the best thing that happened to me since Clinton gave me the briefcase full of money. Nothing was keeping me in Lakewood after I graduated. The world was a big place, and I had seen so little of it. Being in LA also meant I'd have three thousand miles to separate me from Mom. That alone was a beautiful thing. Once I closed the front door on Mom, that was it. I wouldn't budge on cutting Mom out of my life. Even if she gave me the biggest apology in the world. For Mom, there was no forgiveness. She didn't deserve it.

"Yeah. I'll move to LA with you," I said.

"That's all I wanted to hear." Tripp pulled me in for a bear hug before I could blink. He hugged me so tightly my lungs couldn't expand.

"I can't breathe," I said.

"Sorry." Tripp released me. "I didn't realize I was an intense hugger."

"No problem. Just don't do it again."

"Fair enough."

"I'm glad you want me to go to LA with you," I said.

"Not a big deal. It was the next step in our relationship."

Thank goodness Tripp wasn't bored of me. Spending time with him was great, but even I sometimes wondered what he saw in me. Tripp was hot, so he could've had any guy he wanted. Yet he wanted me. And that fact didn't go unnoticed.

"My mother is gonna realize I moved away from home eventually," I said.

"I know, I know."

"But it'll be worth it. I deserve to live my life."

"Amen to that."

"And thank you for agreeing to keep the briefcase here. Don't know what I'd do if my mother found it."

"Please stop worrying so much. It won't do you any good."

Tripp should've known better than to make his comment. Didn't matter if I was seventeen or eighty-seven. I'd always worry. And I once again blamed my fucking mother. No doubt existed in my mind how

I'd be a different person if it wasn't for always wondering when the next bad thing would happen.

"Have you met me?" I asked.

"I never thought my senior year of high school would impact my life so much."

"Me neither."

Tripp squeezed my hand. "I'm glad I met you."

The old me might've once again teased or mocked Tripp for being honest about his feelings. But I couldn't. I wouldn't. Being childish by using teasing to hide my feelings for Tripp was no way to live. Life was just too short for bravado and games.

"Same. Don't know what I'd do without you," I said.

"Would you wanna order a pizza for dinner?" Tripp asked. "I've been craving pizza since the last time we got one."

"That good?" I asked.

"Yup."

I nodded. "Sure. A pepperoni pizza sounds great."

"I'll go grab my iPhone from the kitchen, and order our dinner."

"Perfect."

Tripp left his bedroom without another word, and I was alone.

I shook my head. So much happened in the last year, and I'd always be amazed how it transpired. One minute Declan was alive. The next minute, he wasn't. One minute Gina and I were distant. The next, we were besties again. One minute Tripp refused to forgive me. The next, we mended our relationship.

My mind drifted back to Declan. He deserved to enjoy senior year like Gina, Tripp, and me. Yet no amount of time changed how Declan's death couldn't be undone. And I'd always feel guilty about it. If I hadn't blabbed to Mom about Declan helping me become emancipated, then he might still be alive.

Declan was flawed like everyone else—dealing drugs wouldn't have helped him write an outstanding college essay—but he was still a person. There was nothing more tragic than a young person having his life cut short. His parents and friends were just left with an endless amount of, "What If?" because Declan would never fulfill his potential.

I returned home from school, finding Mom in her usual spot on the couch with her usual table settings.

"Get the fuck over here, boy!" Mom said.

My back hairs rose. It didn't matter if this happened once or a hundred times. I'd never be used to Mom demanding my presence. No telling what she was about to do.

"The fuck do you want?" I asked.

"Don't speak to me in that tone."

"What?"

"I know about your meeting with Clinton and how he handed you a briefcase full of money. And you better start talking, boy! The private investigator provided me with pictures, which I can show you if you don't believe me!" Mom paused for a beat, sucking on her teeth. "Yeah. That's right. I hired a PI to investigate my own son. At this point, you should realize I don't have any boundaries. It's important for me to know what you're up to."

The old me would've winced from Mom discovering something I wanted to keep secret. But not now. Too much happened for me to revert back to being the scared, little boy. Mom might've stolen a lot from me over the years—my dignity, safety, emotional wellbeing—but she wouldn't take one more fucking thing from me. So, I needed to do what I did that weekend when Tripp and I had our weekend. I needed to tell Mom I was moving away from home after graduation, and how there wasn't a fucking thing she could do about it. Nope. Her days of terrorizing me were fucking over.

I folded my arms. "You're absolutely right. Clinton gave me three million dollars, although I'm not stupid enough to reveal where the briefcase is."

"Why would you meet with your faggot father?" Mom rose, then her pupils dilated. "Hasn't he done enough to us? Or maybe you've forgotten about his abandonment?"

There it was. Faggot. The old mom, just begging to come out to play. Maybe that was fine, though. Mom couldn't be a "nice" person forever, so it was best not to waste hers and mine time by pretending to be a good person. She would've had better luck winning the lottery.

"I'm leaving you," I said.

"What the hell are you talking about?"

"I'm moving to LA with Tripp after graduation," I said. "And there isn't a fucking thing you can do to stop me. I'll also be cutting you out of my life once I leave home."

"You're right. I can't do anything to stop you." Mom paused for a second. "But that doesn't mean I can't tell you what I think about you, because it's about time I told you what a spoiled little piece of shit you are."

"Huh?"

Mom shoved me against the wall. And my throat constricted. Having Mom pin me against something was the last thing I needed. No telling what she'd do next. Like if she lit a cigarette and burned me with it.

"I've given you food, shelter, and clothing, yet you continue to be so nasty to me," Mom said. "And that only confirms one of my previous thoughts."

"And what's that?"

"That I should've had an abortion. You've been nothing but a burden and are the worst thing that happened to me."

"Acting like a psychotic bitch is all you—nobody made you behave that way. So, you only have yourself to blame for being lonely and miserable."

"Doubtful." Mom punched me. Over. And over. And over again.

I wouldn't be the boy who tolerated getting smacked by his mother, though. So, I smacked my head against hers. She stumbled backwards before falling on the carpet. And I couldn't help wishing she'd fall onto an object or piece of furniture. Something, anything that could've fatally wounded her. Death was what she deserved.

Tripp and I stood in his kitchen after school.

He just put the brownie tray in the oven, yet I almost laughed. I hadn't helped him much with the preparing and mixing of ingredients. Nope. Instead, I just stared at him. But, maybe, just maybe, that was fine. Tripp hadn't complained about me being useless. Baking brownies was also his idea.

I chuckled. "Gotta admit I'm disappointed."

"What do you mean?"

"It would've been cool if you made 'special' brownies."

"I'm not a stoner."

"Your loss," I said.

He lifted my chin up. "You don't have to make a joke, Colt. Telling your mother about moving away from home after graduation must've terrified you."

Tripp was right. Informing Mom about my post high school plans was a big mistake. But it was better that I got it out of the way. Procrastinating the matter would've only made more dread shoot through my body. And I couldn't have that. Mom already caused me enough sleepless nights.

Tripp looped his arms around me. "I'm proud of you. Hope you know that."

"You don't have to say that."

"Yeah, I do. No offense, but we both know how nobody has ever told you that before."

"True."

"I'm sorry your mother punched you, though." Tripp glanced at the oven for a second. "Can't be easy knowing she's always gonna be cruel."

"Doesn't matter. I have you."

Tripp grinned. "Have you given any thought to what you want for dinner? Pizza or Chinese food are both good options."

"Chinese food is fine—I haven't had that since our weekend getaway all those months ago." I bit my lip. "Unless you want pizza."

"Chinese food works." Tripp sighed. "And I'm sorry we never had another weekend getaway. Life just got in the way."

"Don't worry about it."

The scent of warm chocolate continued wafting through the air. And my stomach growled. Forget about dinner. I wanted to pig out and eat all the brownies. I didn't think I could wait another hour or two for dinner. Not when my stomach was still making noises. There was a chance I'd eat all the brownies before Tripp could have one.

"It's okay if you're disappointed about that," Tripp said. "I promised we'd return at some point."

"The only thing that matters is that we're together."

"Agreed," he said.

The oven timer beeped, then Tripp grabbed mitts. He removed the tray from the oven and placed it on the middle of the stove. Then, he turned the oven off. Tripp took the mitts off and grabbed his iPhone from his pocket.

"I'll order dinner," Tripp said.

"Good."

Tripp gave me a look. "But don't even think about having a brownie before. I can't let you gorge on dessert before dinner."

"Fine.

CHAPTER 23

I returned home from school, finding Mom sitting on the living room couch. But there wasn't a bottle of Beefeater gin or glass on the living room table. Instead, two men sat next to her. And my pulse drummed in my ears. One glance at the gold badge on their belts revealed everything worth knowing. Mom must've been chatting with the police.

My gaze drifted to Mom. Both of her eyes were black and blue. And they looked fresh. She hadn't had them when I left for school this morning.

Mom stood. "Could you please come to the living room, Colton?"

I exhaled a long breath. Best to do what I always did when Mom wanted something from me—chat with her and get it over with. Maybe, just maybe, my life would be okay. It wasn't like I did anything wrong.

"Now," Mom said, raising her voice.

I shuffled to the living room.

The shorter officer stood, then shook my hand. "I'm Detective Miller."

The other detective rubbed his salt and pepper mustache, then rose. "And I'm Detective Roberts."

"What's going on?" I asked.

"We'll ask the questions," Detective Miller said.

Detective Roberts glared at his partner. "You're supposed to be working on being more personable. How do you expect civilians to trust the police if you're gonna give platitude every five seconds?"

"Enough!" Detective Miller exclaimed.

"Am I in trouble?"

Detective Roberts sighed. "We're here to arrest you."

"For what?" I asked.

"Attempted murder," Detective Roberts revealed.

"Of whom?" I asked.

"Me," Mom said.

I quirked my eyebrows. "The fuck are you talking about?"

Detective Miller rolled his eyes. "Do you always use bad language in front of women? If so, then you might wanna re-examine your priorities."

Detective Roberts elbowed his partner. "Let's stick to the facts. We wouldn't wanna give Colton grounds to dismiss the case."

"She's the one who has tried to kill me on numerous occasions!" I exclaimed.

Detective Miller pointed to Mom. "Her black eyes and strangulation marks on her neck say otherwise."

"Huh?" I asked.

Mom pulled back her shirt collar. Detective Miller might not have given a good impression of cops, but he hadn't lied. Mom had strangulation marks around her neck. And I scratched my cheek. I didn't understand why Mom had black eyes and bruise marks.

My pulse reverberated louder and faster through my ears. Wait. There was a simple explanation about how Mom got her injuries. I only needed one guess as to what was going on. Mom must've inflicted the wounds on her neck so she could frame me. Either that or she used makeup to create the wounds. Shit. What a fucking psycho. She couldn't accept I was gonna live happily ever after with Tripp thanks to the money Clinton gave me.

"She's lying. I'd never intentionally hurt her," I said, stuttering. "She's the one who abused me all these years. Go ask Sheriff Down yourself. I once tried to file a police report, but he laughed me out of his office."

Detective Roberts ran his fingers through his pushed back, brown hair. "Yeah, we chatted with Sheriff Down."

"Okay. Good," I said.

"Told us you concocted some abuse scenario because you were bored," Detective Miller said. "And that only confirms what a piece of trash you are. What kind of kid abuses his own mother?"

"You've gotta believe me," I said. "My mother is lying. She did this to herself."

"Why would she do that?" Detective Roberts asked.

"To frame me as her ultimate act of revenge because I'm leaving home once I graduate," I said. "Please believe me."

"Your mother mentioned that," Detective Miller said. "Said that's what made you try to kill her."

"What the fuck?" I asked.

"She was so upset you wanted to move away from home, and only wanted to have a simple conversation with you," Detective Miller said.

"I know my rights—I've got the right to remain silent," I said.

"You're absolutely correct; you've got the right to remain silent." Detective Miller took handcuffs out of his pocket, then waved them at me. "And that's what I'd advise you to do."

Tears pricked my eyes. I couldn't believe it. I was close to getting my happily ever after with Tripp, yet Mom played the long game. Pretending to be nice, only to strike back even more aggressively.

"You know my mother's a drunk, right?" I asked. "You can check her credit card bills, I'm sure you'll find dozens of purchases of Beefeater gin."

Detective Miller shook his head in a vigorous fashion. "Blaming the victim is disgusting. But for your information, yes. Your mother coped with drinking too much and mentioned how she's been trying to cut back on her alcohol intake, which is very admirable."

"Bullshit," I whispered.

Detective Miller put his free hand by his ear. "What was that? Maybe you wanna say that a little louder. I didn't hear you."

Detective Roberts gripped his tie. "Let's get this over with."

"You're under arrest, Colton Foster." Detective Miller walked over to me, then grabbed my hands and forced the handcuffs on me. "You have the right to remain silent. Anything you say can and will be used against you in a court of law. You have the right to an attorney. If you cannot afford an attorney, one will be provided for you."

More tears trickled down my cheeks. Fuck. I was wrong about the universe ever being on my side. The world was a fucked-up place. And maybe, just maybe, I wouldn't have been in this position if I took a more active role in escaping my mother a long time ago. But no. I was some weak, poor kid with no future.

I gave Mom a death glare. "You won't get away with this."

"Please go easy on him," Mom said. "Just want my boy to get the help he needs. Not looking to ruin his life or anything."

"You're such an amazing person," Detective Miller said.

"What a load of fucking bullshit," I said. "Interview my teachers. Or guidance counselors. Or even my boyfriend, Tripp. Then, you'll know the truth about my mother."

"Don't tell us how to do our jobs. We're done here." Detective Miller gripped my wrists tighter before dragging me out of the living room, out the front door, and to the police car parked behind one of the bushes on the left side of my house.

The wind whistled, then rain hammered against the ground. Mom might've won this round. But I wasn't defeated. Not yet. I wasn't gonna be the poor boy who lost his future because his physically, abusive, drunk mother outsmarted him. There had to be a way out of this predicament. I didn't know what I'd do if I went to prison.

I sported an orange jumpsuit, handcuffed while sitting at a table in the Lakewood County jail visitor's room. The guard opened the door, then Tripp walked over to my table and sat next to me.

And my current sadness and anger wouldn't disappear anytime soon. I fought back tears half an hour or so earlier while I stood in the room where they took people's mugshots at the Lakewood County jail.

Crying might've made me human, but I refused to show vulnerability. Especially since Detective Miller was the one taking my mugshot.

My heart ached, and I wasn't embellishing. I wanted nothing more than for Tripp to hug or kiss me, but physical contact wasn't allowed.

I looked away from Tripp. Knowing about my shitty home life was different then Tripp seeing me in my jail uniform and handcuffed. My current predicament made me feel less than human. Like I was some kind of animal. The universe stole what was left of my dignity, and there wasn't a fucking thing I could do.

"Thanks for coming," I murmured.

"You don't have to be ashamed. Please look me in the eye, Colt."

"This is all my fault. I should've never told my mother I was leaving her."

His lips twisted like he ate something sour. "Don't punish yourself too much. Your mother would've eventually discovered you were leaving home."

I remained silent. When Tripp was right, he was right.

"I've already spoken to a lawyer who can represent you at your bail hearing. And he's confident you can get you out on bail. It's your first offense."

"No," I said.

"Don't tell me you're too proud to accept financial help, because I don't want you using the money Clinton gave you to pay for your lawyer. Not when my family is so rich that this isn't even a drop in the bucket."

"It's not about the money."

"Then what?" Tripp asked.

"I'm breaking up with you."

He gasped. "What?"

"It's for your own good. I'm not trying to hurt you."

"That's bullshit, and you know it."

"I don't want our last conversation to be bitter, so please don't raise your voice."

His Adam's apple jumped up and down. "I'm not letting you push me away."

"Doesn't matter—this is what I want," I said. "You deserve better, and your life will be easier without me. You're gonna go to college, meet a nice guy—one who isn't as fucked up as me—and have a great life."

"No," Tripp said, shaking his head. "You can't do this. There are two people involved in this relationship, and I'm not gonna let you give up because you're scared. Don't you get it? You can end the cycle of self-destructive behavior."

"Doesn't matter if I beat these charges," I said. "My mother is gonna keep coming for me no matter what I do. So, I'm setting you free."

Tripp sobbed. "Please don't do this, Colt. You've come so far and deserve a chance at happiness."

"Sorry, but I'm done."

"It's your turn to give me a chance, Colt!" Tripp begged.

"Time's up," the guard by the door said.

The door opened, and another guard entered the visitor's room. He walked over to me, grabbed me, and pulled me away from the table.

Tripp cried louder this time. "This isn't over, Colt. I'm gonna return tomorrow, and we're gonna discuss this."

It was nice knowing someone believed in me. But Tripp should've known better. His life was gonna be so much better without me. Simpler, really. If I somehow got out of this shithole, then it'd be thanks to whatever public defender represented me.

I cocked my head back at Tripp—I was almost by the door now. "Don't bother. Good-bye, Tripp."

Tripp made a fist, then broke out into another fit of hysterical sobs. "I love you, Colt."

The guard watching over the room opened the door. Then, the guard pushed me out of the room. The door clanked shut. Tripp was no longer visible, and the guard corralled me down a hallway.

My cell door clinked open, waking me up.

"You have a new friend," said the guard.

I looked up. A guy in an orange jumpsuit—who must've been well over six foot—stood in my cell.

"Play nice." The guard locked the cell, then left.

My cellmate rubbed his beard before walking towards me. He hovered so close that his body odor prickled my skin.

"I heard the cops talking when I got my mugshot taken," said the guy. "Is it true you're in here for trying to kill your mother?"

"I don't have to justify my life to you." I gave him a dirty look. "Could easily reverse the question and ask what you're in for. But I won't. I don't want trouble."

"Only a low life piece of shit beats up their mother." The man kneeled, then grabbed something from his sock. He lunged forward, jabbing the item in my stomach. He pulled it out, to show me my blood shining on a piece of metal, before sticking in me again.

This was it. My obituary was gonna say I was stabbed in my jail cell before I got a bail hearing. And I only had myself to blame. My fate was sealed a long time ago; I just hadn't realized it.

CHAPTER 24

I yawned and rubbed my eyes. Then, I tried stretching. Except I didn't anticipate the sharp, shooting pain in my abdomen.

Someone snickered. I tilted my head. Sheriff Down sat in a chair in front of my bed. "You might wanna stay put," he said.

"Where the fuck am I?" I asked.

"County jail hospital."

"What the fuck happened?" I demanded.

"You were stabbed three times in your cell and had to get lots of stitches. You're also doped up on pain medicine."

"Why was I stabbed?"

He shrugged. "Don't know. You'd have to ask the person who stabbed you."

"The fuck are you doing here?"

"Nice to see you have a colorful vocabulary."

Now wasn't the time for lecturing me about swearing. It wasn't like we were in church. It wasn't like I did something bad. Like kill someone. Or ignore a child's abuse claim.

I gave him a dirty look. "You didn't answer my question."

"Not every day that somebody gets stabbed at my jail."

My eyebrows knitted together. "Afraid I'm gonna sue?"

"Not exactly."

"Then what?"

He rubbed his mustache—which was more gray than black—then coughed. "I'm inclined to believe you about how you didn't attack and injure your mother."

I must not have heard him correctly. I couldn't believe what I was hearing. And I would've played Lotto if I were eighteen. No telling when I would be this lucky again. Probably never again.

I pursed my lips. "How kind of you."

"The Lakewood County District Attorney is declining to prosecute the case. He also doesn't fully believe your mother."

"Don't care. My mother will just hunt me down and make my life hell."

Sheriff Down chuckled. "What are you talking about? Don't you wanna be released?"

"You're a fucking piece of shit," I said.

He put his hands in his lap. "I don't follow you."

"I'm not the one who is violent with my mother, she's the one who is violent with me." Tears pricked my eyes. "But you're too much of a fucking asshole to realize that. I once visited you to file a police report."

Sheriff Down remained silent.

"But you told me I was mistaken, and threw the report in the trash," I continued.

Sheriff Down tapped his feet against the ground, unable to meet my gaze.

I grunted. "Do you remember that day or not?"

"Yes," he whispered.

"You could've helped me, you fucking piece of shit."

"I'm sorry."

"That's all you have to say?" I spat.

"What do you want me to do?"

"My mother killed Declan Price. Only problem is I don't have enough evidence."

"What did you just say?" Sheriff Down asked.

"You gotta help me," I said.

He cackled. "I'm not so sure about that."

"I want you to let people think I'm dead. You're the only one who has met with me besides my doctors, right?"

Sheriff Down nodded.

"If my mother thinks I'm dead, then that might drive her insane enough to confess to Declan's murder," I said.

"But you're claiming she treats you like shit."

"Abusing me is her whole world. And imagine if she didn't have that anymore?"

He raised his eyebrows. "Where the hell am I supposed to stash you?"

I rolled my eyes. It really was impossible to like him. He was the Sheriff, not me. And if he wanted to keep his job, then he needed to take the initiative. "At a cheap motel or safe house," I said. "I can't be the first person the Lakewood Police Department has put in hiding."

"You would abandon your whole life?" he asked.

"Doesn't matter," I forced out.

His jaw lowered. "What about Tripp? Aren't you dating him?"

Anger shot through my veins. Sheriff Down shouldn't have mentioned Tripp.

I narrowed my gaze. "How the fuck do you know that?"

"It's my job to ask questions."

My mouth gaped. "Oh."

"You didn't answer my question."

"Tripp and I had our final goodbye, so I'm good." I scratched an itch on the back of my neck. "Told him to let me go when we chatted in the visitor room. I'm just a complication—Tripp deserves to have a good life without any drama"

"What if your mother never confesses?" Sheriff Down asked. "And what if she comes to collect your remains?"

My head pounded some more. Sheriff Down was too much. One or two questions was understandable, yet a picture of him would've been next to the word, "buzzkill" in the dictionary. Because that was what Sheriff Down was. He sucked the joy out of everything.

"We'll worry about that when the time comes," I said. "As for my remains, just say there was a mix-up and you accidentally cremated me."

He blinked. "You really want this?"

"Yes."

"Fine, I'll agree to this plan." His shoulders shook. "It's the least I owe you after everything that happened."

Nice knowing he was still human, and could express contrition like any decent person.

"Thanks," I said.

"But don't go acting cocky," he said. "Not like I'm gonna apologize. Anyone would've had a hard time believing your abuse allegations."

"Whatever helps you sleep at night."

EPILOGUE

TRIPP

I always knew Colton's mother would be the death of him. I just didn't know how or when. If I had, then I would've saved Colton from being stabbed in his jail cell. And Colton's death was why tears welled in my eyes while I stood in front of the bedroom mirror adjusting my tie.

My throat burned. I couldn't believe it. The boy who I loved was gone, and there wasn't anything I could do to undo Colt's death. I could try to rationalize the situation until it consumed me, though. I should've done something to protect Colton from his mother. More specifically, go with him to the police and file a new police report even though his previous time didn't go well. Or even tell a teacher—someone who was familiar with Colton, like Mr. Hopper. Colton didn't deserve to die at seventeen. He had his whole life ahead of him, and death was a thief.

Someone knocked on my bedroom door. I wiped the tears from my eyes before cocking my head. Mom stood at the entrance of my bedroom.

"Can I come in?" Mom asked.

I nodded. "Sure."

Mom shuffled over to me, then stood behind him. After that, she adjusted my tie. I didn't flinch or protest, though. Having Mom fix my tie was cute. It was something to focus on besides Colt's death.

Mom sighed. "I know words are empty, but I'm sorry about Colton."

"Thanks," I whispered.

She rested her hands on my shoulders. "For what it's worth, Colton was lucky to have you. It's good he got to know some happiness. So, hold onto that."

"He's fucking dead, Mom."

Mom didn't respond. Instead, she bit her lip. I didn't blame her for silence, though. Nothing she said changed how Colton was dead. And she could've been angry about me cursing. I couldn't imagine that made her happy.

I looked down. "Sorry for swearing."

"Don't apologize on my account. It's important for you to purge your feelings." She gripped my shoulders tighter. "Just shocked you're going to the funeral."

"I'm not afraid of his mother."

"Your father and I would be happy to come with you."

My mother was being ridiculous. I was capable of doing things by myself. Having my parents attend Colton's funeral also wouldn't change anything. Like how I might accost Colton's mother at the funeral. That monster didn't deserve forgiveness. Nope. Being told how fucking terrible her actions were was the only thing she deserved.

"This is something I've gotta do myself," I said.

"Understood."

I sighed in relief. I didn't know what I would've done if Mom insisted she and Dad accompany me to the funeral. Because I didn't feel like arguing. Not now. No point in bickering with my parents. Not when Colt was dead.

I sobbed louder. "The whole situation fucking sucks. Colt's mother is gonna get away with everything."

"There's another way to look at it," Mom said.

I lifted my gaze. "Don't tell me to be positive."

"I'm not."

"Then what?" I asked.

"You can get satisfaction from how miserable Colton's mother is."

I shot her a confused look. "She didn't care about him."

"That's not my point. Deep down, his mother must be a very unhappy person. She has nothing in her life."

I grinned. Mom was right no matter how morbid the idea sounded. Colton's mother had to be really miserable. It was the only thing that'd get me through Colton's funeral.

"True," I said.

Mom gritted her teeth. "Eventually, the pain will lessen."

"I want Colt back."

Mom exhaled a longer breath. "That's cute you had a nickname for him."

"Colton never had a fair chance." I tucked my hands into my blazer pockets. "All because of his fucking mother. Well, that fucking bitch isn't gonna get away with this."

"Be careful, sweetheart."

"Please don't lecture me," I said. "His mother didn't even claim his body, so that means the morgue cremated his remains."

Gray clouds lingered in the sky after I exited my car and walked to the church's sidewalk.

I lucked out, though. I was now face to face with Colton's mother. And it was time to give that bitch a taste of her own medicine.

She glared at me. "Tripp."

"Hello, Abby."

"What the fuck are you doing here?" she asked. "Your dumb faggot ass doesn't deserve to be here."

"I'm not afraid of you, bitch!" I exclaimed.

She almost choked. "Come again?"

"You heard me. And I'm gonna decimate you. You made Colton's life Hell, and you aren't gonna get away with that."

"You've got some nerve talking to me like this." She wrinkled her nose. "And you're lucky I haven't banned you from attending his funeral. Colton's situation says more about you, not me."

"What do you mean?" I stammered.

"You could've helped him, yet you did nothing. If you cared about him, then you would've gotten him away from me. But I'm sure he was just some piece of ass to you."

What a psychotic maniac. Abby couldn't have said what she just did. Only an evil person would blame someone else for the pain they inflicted on someone.

"I loved Colton with all my heart, and that was more than can be said about you," I said.

"I gave him food and shelter."

"We both know that isn't entirely true."

"Excuse me?" she asked.

I scoffed. "He spent a lot of his free time with me. So, I gave him more shelter than you."

"You wish."

"Do you even care that he's dead?"

She grunted. "It's not a matter of not caring. It's a matter of not giving a fuck. Getting stabbed in his cell was Colton's punishment for being a faggot."

Abby was unbelievable. The normal response would've been to take a break from her bigotry or even to be silent. But no. This woman would hang on to her hatred till her last dying breath. Apparently, some people were that spiteful.

"You fucking bitch." I moved my hand forward so I could slap her. But she grabbed my wrist before I struck her cheek. I wasn't mad, though. I smacked her with my other hand.

She rubbed her cheek. Red coated her fingers.

Awesome. I made her bleed, and I wouldn't apologize for doing so. It wasn't like I killed her in broad daylight. She just needed to know her behavior towards Colt wasn't okay.

I leaned closer, lips brushing against her right ear. "And don't forget I know you killed Declan."

Abby cackled. "Prove it."

"Don't have to. Whether or not you go to prison, the truth will come out, and you'll have to live with the consequences." I leaned back from Abby before spitting in her face. "That's for Colton. And I hope you burn in Hell, you fucking bitch."

I finished getting my stuff from my locker Monday morning when I bumped into Warren.

I didn't expect to bump into Declan's best friend. Perhaps he wanted to pay his respects to Colton. Doing so would've been the polite thing to do.

He tugged at the sides of his varsity jacket. "Just wanted to say that I'm sorry for your loss. Can't imagine what you must be going through."

I exhaled a breath. "Thanks. I appreciate it."

"The guys on the football team made me find you."

I would've laughed if life wasn't so morbid. I should've known Warren wouldn't chat with me because he came up with the idea. This was the same guy who Colt sparred with when he looked into that rumor about Declan dealing drugs.

I shrugged. "Okay."

"That doesn't mean I'm not sorry—I am. Everyone else was simply too weak to give you their condolences."

"Colton is dead, Warren."

His Adam's apple bobbed. "If you need anything, then let me or the guys know. You don't deserve to suffer in silence."

I couldn't get over Colt's death. Tragedies weren't supposed to happen in small towns like the one I lived in.

"His abuse was an open secret, and I didn't do a fucking thing!" I exclaimed.

"Why?"

"I couldn't alienate him. If I pushed him too hard, then he'd have nobody."

"That sounds smart."

"I should've taken out a hit on his mother. Or hired a lawyer to get him emancipated. None of this had to happen."

"Don't punish yourself too much. Colton wouldn't have wanted that."

"You didn't know a fucking thing about him."

Warren didn't say anything. Instead, he frowned. Damn. I shouldn't have made such a rude remark. Even if my grief might mean having childish, contradictory, or unexpected reactions. If I was gonna deal with my emotions, then I was gonna need someone. Anyone who would let me bitch about how unfair life was.

"He was stolen from me," I said, raising my voice.

"I'm sorry, man." Warren hugged me, and I didn't shove him away. At least he tried being supportive. Better than doing nothing.

The chattering of numerous voices filled VERONICA'S a couple of weeks later while I sat at a table, drinking a caramel latte. And I wasn't alone. Colt's best friend, Gina, was across from me.

How Gina plastered a smile to her face was beyond me, though.

Sure. My life would eventually get better. But none of that mattered now. Not when Colt's death was still fresh in my mind.

She stretched her hands out on the table. "Thanks for meeting with me. I wasn't sure you'd be receptive to this when we exchanged phone numbers at the funeral"

"No offense, but I'm not sure how I can help you."

"You were the person Colton loved most."

"The whole thing is all my fault," I said.

Her eyebrows inched up. "I don't follow."

"I should never have let his bad home life go on this long. If I did one thing different, then that might've changed everything."

A couple of tears fell down her face. "Maybe it'd be helpful to talk about the positive memories about Colton. Like a support group."

"Whatever." I sipped my beverage, then pressed the mug against my face. The warmth soothed my cheeks, and I couldn't help sighing in relief. The calendar might've said it was the first week of June. But it might as well have been the middle of March. The distinct chill permeating the air from the rain, dampness, and below average temperatures was just that vindictive. I should've worn a jacket for my meeting with Gina. At least then I wouldn't have been shivering and my teeth wouldn't have been chattering.

"I can go first if you want," Gina said.

"Sure."

"I don't know if you remember, but you and Colton stole a gaze at each other last fall. In fact, Colton and I were sitting at this table when you two locked eyes."

"I remember."

"Colton was nervous when he saw you, and I made him tell me everything. He even confided in me about his sexuality."

"Why are you telling me this?" I asked.

"Thought it was cute how this tough guy had a weakness. And he was also scared as shit about whether you'd accept his apology."

"I didn't—not at first."

Gina squeezed my hand. "That was really good of you to give him a chance."

"I saw a real person under his façade. A scared little boy who wanted to be loved."

"And it's thanks to you that Colton knew what it's like to be loved." She chugged the rest of her coffee. "Just a shame it ended abruptly."

I could see why Gina was a good friend for Colton. At least I was a positive force in Colt's life. I couldn't imagine what Colt's life would've been like if he hadn't met me or I hadn't forgiven him. His life would've ended tragically, only worse. Colt would've died thinking nobody loved him if he had nobody in his life.

"Would it be okay if I shared a memory now?" I asked.

Colt wasn't just her childhood best friend. He was the love of my life, and I'd never forget that. Even if some people would've judged me for being attached to a dead person. There was just no denying the impact Colt and I had on each other. Like with how my heart fluttered from the first second we made eye contact in that bedroom at Declan's party. She didn't even blink. "Sure."

"Why don't I tell you about the weekend trip Colton and I once took together?"

Gina beamed her eyes. "Bet it's a good story."

I downed my caramel latte while I fought back tears. Not because I was too upset to reminisce but because of what I was drinking. Caramel lattes were Colt's favorite beverage. And stuff like that was the only reminder I had left of him.

I ran into Mr. Hopper one more morning the following week after my coffee hangout with Gina. And I almost walked away from him when he placed a hand on my shoulder. "Do you have a second?" he asked.

I coughed into my arm. "Sure."

"Wanted to extend my sympathy." He pushed his glasses further up his nose. "Teens hate it when adults pretend to know how they feel or think, so I won't psychoanalyze you. But you should know I'm sorry for your loss."

"Thanks. It's so unfair." I tugged my backpack strap tighter. "I can't stop thinking how Colt had his whole life ahead of him, and how he's missing out on prom, graduation, moving away from home."

"I lost my sister when I was your age."

Wow. Of all the things I expected to happen, I didn't expect Mr. Hopper to reveal a similarity. I never once considered how students and teachers had things in common.

"How did you get over it?" I asked.

Mr. Hopper didn't respond. Instead, he pulled out a cloth from his pocket and wiped his glasses after a couple of tears fell down his face.

The warning bell screeched while students and teachers flooded the hallway, yet neither of us moved.

"Didn't mean to overstep," I continued.

"You didn't."

"It's okay. You don't have to answer my question."

Mr. Hopper's lips quivered while a couple of more tears rolled down his cheeks. "Never got over my sister's death. Just learned to live with it."

I almost had a heart attack when I returned home from school one week after my chat with Mr. Hopper.

I couldn't believe who stood at the opposite end of my bedroom. No amount of blinking changed the identity of the guy I was looking at. Yet it couldn't be him. Dead people didn't walk with the living.

"Colt?" I stammered.

He sighed. "Gonna hug me, or what?"

I ran over to Colt and gave him a bear hug without hesitation. Colton was really pressed against my body, which meant I couldn't have hallucinated him.

"How are you alive?" I asked after we detached from our embrace a couple of minutes later. "You were stabbed to death and cremated? And how'd you get into my house?"

"Yes, it's true I was stabbed." Colt paused for a beat. "As for how I got into your home, I haven't forgotten about the spare key under the mat by the front door.""

"I still don't understand how you're alive."

"I survived and was rushed to the infirmary."

"Okay?"

"That's when I chatted with Sheriff Down," Colt revealed. "I convinced him to let people think I was dead."

"Why?" I demanded. "And don't give me some nonsense about how you think you're too broken and damaged to be loved."

He shook his head in a vigorous fashion. "You just don't understand."

"Then please clue me in?"

"I wanted to drive my mother insane," he said. "She might be a monster, but she's still human. And I'm sorry, but you can't deny how your life would be a lot simpler without me in it—I'm just a complication"

"What the hell is that supposed to mean?" I snapped, pulse blaring in my ears. Just couldn't believe Colt let him think he died. I thought I meant more to him than some twisted idea that seemed ripped from a soap opera.

"I wanted to drive my mother crazy from the guilt in hopes that would make her confess to Declan's murder. And it worked. You can watch the evening news tonight and see that I'm correct. The Lakewood Police Department is planning a press conference."

I clenched my jaw. "Do you have any idea what it was like thinking you were dead?"

"I'm sorry," he murmured.

"Apologizing doesn't fix everything. What about Gina? Were you okay with her also thinking you were dead?"

"Not like we saw each other that much."

I crossed my arms. "She was your childhood best friend, Colt."

"I know."

My pulse didn't lower. If anything, the tingling sensation in my hands and toes intensified.

I wouldn't deny how Colt being alive was a good thing. He could now live the rest of his life like he intended. But I couldn't get over him letting me think he was dead. And I wasn't being cruel; I was being honest. If he really loved me, then he would've clued me in on the plan. It wasn't like I would've snitched on him. I had nothing to gain by betraying him. If anything, I would've been happy to help him. Or visit him. I couldn't imagine Colt enjoyed being tucked away in isolation at whatever cheap motel or safe house Sheriff Down stashed him away at. And that was bullshit about Colt thinking he made life too dramatic. If I didn't like him, then I wouldn't date him.

His eyes bulged. "What? Can't forgive me?"

"It's not that simple," I said.

"I wasn't trying to be cruel. I was stabbed first and the plan to 'die' came second."

"I believe you." I paused for a beat. "But that doesn't change how you hurt me, Colt."

"Nice knowing you." Colt smacked my shoulder, then I gripped his arm.

My stomach sank while I remained shocked. It was a shame that Colton reverted back to his old self by trying to push me away. Feelings weren't mutually exclusive. I could be both angry about him not cluing me in on the plan and still love him. And it was unfortunate that my words came back to haunt me. I was the one who once mentioned to Colt about how progress wasn't always linear and people sometimes regressed back to past behavior.

"I'm not saying we can't return to the way things were, but I need time to think things over. Hopefully, you understand that."

"That's fair."

"I'm sorry for you being stabbed, though. That couldn't have been easy."

"It was three times."

"Sorry." I inhaled another deep breath. I had to ask the question that popped into my head no matter how difficult it was. If Colt and I were ever gonna reunite, then I needed to know all the facts. Including the ugly ones. "Did you let yourself get stabbed because you wanted to die? You might not be athletic, but you've always struck me as someone who can hold their own in a fight."

Colt hung his head in shame, avoiding eye contact. "I'll admit. A part of me would've been glad to die. Then, I would've been free of my mother."

I snorted. "I could've helped you with your home situation if you hadn't been so stubborn."

"I know, I know."

My eyebrows knitted together. "Why show up if you think you're not good enough for me and bring too much chaos into my life?"

Colt shrugged. "It's possible for me to still love you, yet realize you deserve better."

Five Months Later

The key clinked in the lock, then I entered my apartment.

The aroma of cheese, tomato, and other herbs wafted through the air, hugging my nostrils. I placed my athletic bag on the mahogany table by the front door. I walked towards the dining room. A plate and wine glass were by both mine and Colt's seats in addition to how a bottle of wine was between our seats. We were lucky that there was a nearby liquor store that didn't bother carding.

"I hope it was okay, but I didn't feel like cooking." Colt smiled, then gave me a quick kiss.

"That's fine. Pizza sounds great."

"How was football practice?" he asked.

"Good."

Colt laughed. "That's all you have to say?"

I shrugged. "I didn't expect to attend college in Los Angeles."

"You aren't mad about not going to Savannah College of Art of Design, are you?"

"No. Being here with you is where I belong. This way I can play football and lacrosse for a division one school, but still get a BA in Photography."

"Makes sense."

I winked. "What about you? How was your day?"

"It was good. I read short story submissions."

Colt wasn't only watching television or playing video games all day. He got a fellowship working for an online literary magazine, which was great. Attending college wasn't the only way to be successful.

"Anything promising?" I asked.

"A few good short stories, but I need to think about them more."

"Fair enough." I sucked in a breath. "There's been something I've been wanting to mention, but I didn't wanna offend you."

He chuckled. "Just say whatever you wanna say."

"We haven't discussed your mother's death."

"There's nothing to dwell on," he said. "There's a certain irony to how we both got stabbed in prison, but I lived, and she died."

Colt's comment might've been demented, but he had a point. Him surviving being stabbed in jail while his mother dying showed there was some justice in the world. I mean, I would've relished her death if I was Colt. She didn't even make it to her trial.

His mother insisted on having a trial despite confessing to Declan's murder. Although she didn't have much of a case. Not when her confession would've been entered as evidence against her.

My mouth gaped. "True."

"And it's not like she can return to haunt me. That was the beauty about identifying her dead body at the morgue. She's absolutely, positively dead." He sighed. "Anyway, can we change the subject?"

I snickered. Colt's thoroughness was one of the things I loved most about him. Only he would make a comment about being certain his mother was dead. I would've hated his mother continuing to hang over him. Colt suffered enough hardships to last several lifetimes. So, it was time for him to be happy. If something bad had to happen, then it could occur to someone else. Someone who deserved to reap the misfortune they sowed.

"Sure. Anything exciting happen to you today?" I asked.

"Gina returned my message—she wants to visit next weekend," Colt revealed. "But I told her I'd have to run it by you first."

"Next weekend is fine."

Colt grinned. "Cool."

"How about we eat the pizza before it gets cold?" I asked.

"Sounds good."

We both sat, then started eating pizza and enjoying our Moscato.

I smiled. Life was beyond messy and complicated, but it was worth living. Colt and I made it past the difficult part—his shitty home life. So, we'd be okay. I just knew it. If a challenge arose, then we'd work through it together. And Colt knew that. Honest communication was one of the conditions of me taking him back.

He grabbed another slice of pizza, then furrowed a brow. "Everything okay?"

"Yeah, everything is just fine."

COLTON

Tripp's lips quivered. "You know you can always be honest with me, right?"

I nodded. "Yeah. But what's your point?"

"I don't expect life to be perfect despite how your mother's no longer an obstacle."

"And I appreciate that." I adjusted my posture in my seat at the table. "But I'm not worried about the rest of my life right now."

He finished his slice of pizza. "You aren't?"

"Nope. The only thing that matters is that I'm happy in this moment."

Tripp chuckled. "I'm impressed."

"How so?"

"The old you would've never said something like that."

"I'm not the same person you met at the party the night Declan died."

My heart lurched. It didn't matter how much time passed since Declan died—I'd never forget about him. Declan was a friend to me when he didn't have to be. And I'd never be okay with how his life ended too soon.

It was interesting, really. My senior year of high school began with a quest to uncover the truth about Declan, yet I became more and more consumed by my relationship with Tripp. But maybe that was okay. Perhaps my relationship with Tripp was Declan's final gift—something that ensured I wouldn't be alone. The idea that Declan was watching over me comforted me.

Tripp's Adam's apple throbbed. "No, you're not."

I wasn't putting on a façade for Tripp—I meant every word I said. My current joy from Tripp was the only thing that mattered. If I continued worrying about when the next bad thing would happen, then I'd miss out on the little moments like this meal with Tripp. And that would've been tragic. Because life really was about the smaller, everyday events as much as it was about the big milestones.

Also available from *Willow River Press*

Meet Connor and Liam in…

LOVE HIM HATE HIM

Evelyn Sinclair was everywhere and nowhere.

Like when I was chatting with her by her locker one second, and the next she'd disappeared. Or when Evelyn made a cryptic remark and the comment stayed with me longer than it should've. Or when I sat in the backseat of Gavin's car. I was next to my friend, Natalie, and Gavin was driving while Mona sat beside him in the passenger seat. Evelyn wasn't in the car, yet her name had come up a dozen times in the last five minutes.

I sighed. "Ending our friendship with Evelyn seems extreme."

Gavin took his eyes off the road for a beat. "Easy for you to say, Connor. You're the only one Evelyn hasn't hurt."

"How'd you feel if you were Natalie, and Evelyn had outed *your* secret crush to the whole school?" Mona asked.

My shoulders tensed. "Wouldn't happen. I don't like anyone."

Mona scoffed. "I've seen the intense eye contact between you and Liam. Can't make that up."

Sweat clung to my brow. Mona was too close to the truth. If I wasn't careful, then she might figure out about last spring.

"What are you saying?" I asked.

"Nothing." Mona unzipped her purse, then grabbed her lipstick and coated her lips with a bright shade of purple.

I loosened my seatbelt. "Outing the crush was cruel, but why ditch Evelyn now? It isn't like she hasn't made mistakes before. Like snitching to Gavin's lacrosse coach about his steroids, or ratting out Mona to her English teacher last spring..."

"You're proving my point," Mona interrupted. "Have you forgotten what happened after Evelyn tattled about my plagiarism?"

I bit my lip. "I'm sure failing English and attending summer school couldn't have been easy..."

"No shit," Mona said. "Try being grounded the summer before your junior year of high school."

"But Evelyn wasn't lying—you plagiarized your English essay," I pointed out.

Mona threw a glance at me, her glare accentuating her menacing green eyes. "Whose side are you on?"

I was right, though. If Evelyn was beyond redemption, then she wouldn't have cared about honesty.

Gavin honked at the driver in front of us, then turned left and barreled down a new street. "I don't know what you see in Evelyn, man."

"Someone doing one bad thing doesn't mean they're evil," I said.

"Maybe in fiction," Mona said.

Gavin grunted after the traffic light turned green. "You didn't answer my question. I wanna know why you bother with Evelyn."

I wiped my palms on my shorts. "She was the first person who accepted my bisexuality. It gave me the confidence to come out."

"That doesn't change the fact that Evelyn is an awful person," Gavin said. "Plus, eighth grade was a long time ago."

"We could've finished our food before leaving," I changed the subject. "Kind of wasteful."

"Only you'd think about food right now," Mona muttered.

"A twenty-minute delay wouldn't have mattered," I replied, resisting the urge to raise my voice. As much as I hated admitting the truth, Mona was probably right. Food was the least of our concerns, even though it really did matter to me. I was a foodie – there was just nothing more comforting than a good meal.

"I'm more interested in Mona's comment about Liam." Gavin paused at a stop sign before making a right turn and driving down a new road.

"Maybe you should leave it alone," Mona said.

"Connor was squirming," Gavin chimed in.

"If you've got something to say, then say it," I said.

"Are you hoping being friends with Evelyn will give you an in with Liam since he's her twin brother?" Gavin asked.

I shook my head several times. "Liam isn't gay or bi."

"He's never had a girlfriend, let alone bragged about a crush," Gavin pointed out.

"So?" I asked.

Gavin looked at me for a fleeting second. "The other guys on the lacrosse team and football team have."

"Lots of people are single in high school," I said.

"Single, yes—celibate, not so much," Gavin countered. "And then there's Liam's constant need to spout homophobic shit."

My stomach lurched. It was impossible to fathom that what Gavin was implying was actually true. But if Liam had never made a racy comment about a girl and was constantly making homophobic comments, then there really was only one logical conclusion. I wouldn't speak the conclusion into existence, though—I couldn't. Not after what had transpired with Liam, because that secret would die with me. Secrecy was just simpler. This way, I couldn't get my feelings hurt again.

I snorted. "You haven't made your point."

"Forget it," Gavin said.

I sniggered. "Have you forgotten I hate Liam?"

Mona giggled. "You never told us what went on between you two."

"That's my prerogative," I said.

I wrinkled my nose. "Have it your way."

Natalie leaned into my right ear. "Everything okay?"

I dug my nails into my palms, almost drawing blood. Didn't matter if Natalie hadn't meant anything by her comment. Fleeting guilt overcame me—she was displaying more politeness for me than I had for her. I should've been more furious with Evelyn for outing Natalie's crush to the entire school. But I couldn't eliminate Evelyn from my life. Not yet, at least. Doing so seemed unfair. Youthful indiscretions—like the unkind things Evelyn had done—happened to most people. Whether people accepted the truth or not, a lot of people did stuff they weren't proud of when they were kids or teenagers—stuff they'd just have to live with.

"Yes," I forced out. "Anyway, there's something you haven't considered yet. Being pissed at Evelyn is one thing, but don't forget about all the good stuff she's done. Have you forgotten all the parties we've attended because of her?"

"Not our fault if you're lonely," Gavin said.

Mona gave Gavin a dirty look but didn't speak.

"Sorry." Gavin shifted in his seat. "Shouldn't have said that."

I ran my fingers through my gel-slicked hair. "Doesn't matter. But... I mean, have you guys ever considered there might be an explanation for the questionable things Evelyn does?"

Most people might not have bothered defending Evelyn to Gavin, Mona, and Natalie, but I tried. This way, I knew I was doing everything I could.

"Really gonna play the dead mommy card?" Mona asked. "Evelyn's gotta become an adult at some point."

"Losing a parent early in life isn't fun," I said.

"And we're sorry your father died, but a parent's death doesn't excuse shitty behavior," Gavin said.

I whipped my head back and forth. "I never said it did; just trying to give context."

Gavin coughed. "More like enabling."

I pressed my head against the car window while a gust of wind pushed a pile of red, orange, and yellow leaves down the road. It was hard to believe it was already the second week of September. Some trite ideas were true no matter how corny they sounded, like that time moved faster than anticipated.

Time. There was something nobody ever had enough of. Like my father. My life had just been beginning when he passed. And I couldn't help thinking about all this time I wouldn't have with my dad. More specifically, the memories he wouldn't share with me. Like prom. Or high school graduation. Or college graduation. Or me starting a career.

"Let's not fight." Natalie flipped her auburn hair over her shoulders. "Evelyn would want that."

"I still can't get over her name," Mona said. "What kind of parent names their kid Evelyn? It's like something from the 1930s."

"Are you kidding?" I asked.

Mona shrugged. "It was an honest question."

"You can keep being Evelyn's friend if you want," Gavin returned to the original topic. "But if you do, you can't be our friend."

"That's harsh," Natalie piped up.

Thank goodness for Natalie. If I was right, she had a future as a diplomat. Most people wouldn't have bothered to show the level-headedness she did.

"Natalie has a point," Mona said. "He can be friends with Evelyn—he just can't discuss her in front of us. What would we ever do without Connor's insightful commentary?"

"Whatever," Gavin muttered.

"What about the football team now and the lacrosse team in the spring?" I asked. "Liam might mention Evelyn at some point."

"And I'll deal with it when he does," Gavin said.

"Evelyn might be a lot of things, but she isn't stupid. There's no way she's gonna be surprised by this conversation," Mona said.

"What do you mean?" I asked.

Mona remained silent for a beat. "She got a 4.0 GPA last year."

I bit my lip, stopping myself from laughing—sensitivity was necessary if I didn't wanna start more trouble. "Admit it—you're jealous of her."

Mona grimaced. "Duh. Why else do you think she'd betray Gavin and me? She wanted Gavin for herself."

"I'm thankful the coach just benched me for the last couple games of the season; could've been a lot worse." Gavin made a left turn, then sped faster when the car behind us kept tailgating.

"Feel like us not calling or texting first is odd, though," Mona said.

I sniffed. Little late for Mona to express doubt after joining with Gavin to crucify me for empathizing with Evelyn.

"Better this way," Natalie said. "She won't see it coming."

The clunky sound of Gavin's ignition halted after he parked by the curb of Evelyn's house.

We undid our seatbelts and got out.

Except I—like Mona, Natalie, and Gavin—didn't bother trekking up Evelyn's driveway. A person sporting a paramedic jacket was pushing a stretcher toward an ambulance. I made a fist as the paramedic glanced down at the body bag, only to shake his head. The bag was partially opened, revealing a portion of the occupant's head. It was Evelyn—I would've recognized her jet-black hair anywhere.

I kicked my feet against the ground, and when the paramedic put the stretcher inside the vehicle, Gavin had to restrain me from darting over to the ambulance. Evelyn was dead. We'd come to her house to end our friendship with her, and she was dead. My throat burned. Her life had been cut short. Dad's time had run out, and so had Evelyn's. And I couldn't help wondering about the future experiences Evelyn would never enjoy. Because Evelyn's mistakes seemed insignificant now. She was still human and hadn't deserved death.

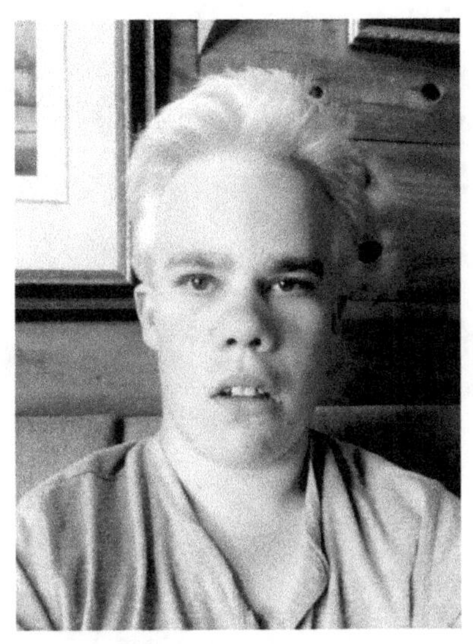

Chris Bedell's previous publishing credits include Thought Catalog, Entropy Magazine, Chicago Literati, and Foliate Oak Literary Magazine, among others. His 2019 books include his NA Thriller BURNING BRIDGES (BLKDOG Publishing), YA Paranormal Romance DEATHLY DESIRES (Deep Hearts YA), and YA Thriller COUSIN DEAREST (BLKDOG Publishing). In addition to his YA Thriller BETWEEN LOVE AND MURDER, his 2020 books include his YA Contemporary I'LL SEE YOU AGAIN (Deep Hearts YA), YA Thriller THE FABULIST (BLKDOG Publishing), YA Thriller I KNOW WHERE THE BODIES ARE BURIED (BLKDOG Publishing), and YA SciFi DYING BEFORE LIVING (Deep Hearts YA). Besides his YA Thriller LOVE HIM/HATE HIM, Chris's 2021 books include his YA Fantasy CROSSING DESIRES (Spectrum Books) and rerelease of his YA Fantasy IN THE NAME OF MAGIC from JMS Books. Furthermore, Chris graduated with a BA in Creative Writing from Fairleigh Dickinson University in 2016.

www.ingramcontent.com/pod-product-compliance
Lightning Source LLC
Chambersburg PA
CBHW062309200726
48292CB00004BA/1437